THE DANCE WE DO IN THE DARK

JANUARY KELLY

Cover design: Black Widow Designs.

Published by: Wandering Reads Press, LLC

ISBN Paperback: 979-8-9916267-6-7
ISBN E-Book: 979-8-9916267-7-4

Wandering Reads
PRESS

Contents

Trigger Warnings and other things

While our characters in this book have their traumas, [see list below] I feel like this is the place where I can also help a friend out with the names in this book. Look, I LOVE a great name that calls to mind a specific person the next time you hear it. But, I also know how utter annoying it can be to Google it so you know you're hearing it correctly in your head.

For you, my friend, I won't leave you hanging.

Trigger Warnings:

- Childhood neglect [referenced, not depicted]

- Violent childhood abuse [referenced, not depicted]

- Stalking

- Death of a parent

- Explicit Sexual Content

Other things:

Ioan: Yo-ann or Yo-n [hard n]

For the you all still struggling to come out of your shell and find *the one*.
Your person is out there...
Jump in with both feet
and dance in the dark.

She lay in the dark and knew everything. —Ian McE-
wan

Prologue-Alyssa

I raised my wrist to my mouth where the wireless microphone was discreetly disguised as a smart watch. I had no idea if my partner, Fox, could hear me on the other end or not, but I shouted into the mic anyway. "Target is weaving in the crowd. I've got eyes on him."

This far away from the stage, the throngs of people were thinner, and it was easier to maneuver between the concertgoers. On a normal night, I might be inclined to take in the show, but this wasn't an ordinary night. My team and I were on a mission to save a sixteen-year-old girl from a trafficker she met online. Her father, a well-known heart surgeon, and his socialite second wife, paid Onyx Industries, the security firm I work for, a large sum of money to keep the girl from making contact and bring her home. Little did I know that her meeting with him would be at an Obliterate show.

Kids are so stupid at this age.

I wove closer to the stage, never losing sight of my target and always only a few feet away. Inching closer every few seconds, the throngs of people began pushing and swaying to the thunderous music. The crowd erupted into a cacophony of cheers and screams as the song ended and a new one immediately began. The bodies around me moved in waves as the mass pushed its way closer to the stage. Deciding this was the ideal time to make contact, I let myself be swept away in the moment, but I never took my eyes off him.

The sound of breakneck guitar riffs and bass vibrated in my bones as I felt tossed like a rag doll through the crowd. I used the force of the human wave to launch myself in the direction I needed to go. My eyes hadn't left my target for a moment, so I was surprised to find, after being able to break free of the tsunamic mob, I was one row off the gated barrier directly center stage.

There he was.

I watched him for what felt like an hour, but it was most definitely only about twenty seconds. He wasn't a bad-looking guy; on the contrary, he was handsome. His dark hair barely touched his shoulders and had a well-groomed look to it. Observing him as he took in the show, the music pounding in his chest just like mine, the colored lights bounced off his tanned face, and he smiled as he sang along. I stepped forward, putting my hand on his shoulder.

"I'm so sorry," I giggled as if he could hear me over the deafening music.

He leaned into my ear, "Why are you following me?"

I wrinkled my nose as cutely as I could, "What are you talking about? Are you as drunk as I am?"

He eyed me suspiciously as I stumbled for effect. I had no idea he had clocked me and I had to save my cover. The only reason I made it this far was because the local LEO's didn't want to involve the Feds and made an agreement with Onyx to apprehend the suspect after we had the girl safe and sound. Getting her was easy; we snatched the naive princess at the door an hour ago.

Grabbing me by the upper arm, he spun me around and pulled my back into his chest. "I know you were following me," he growled and sniffed my hair. "You smell sweet and like a cop. Why don't I show you a real *party*, officer."

I felt his dick stiffen.

Gross.

"First, I'm not a cop," I grinned. "And second, I like a man with a much bigger stick!" With one quick movement, I snapped the back of my head directly into his nose. Blood sprayed like a burst pipe from his face as I whirled around to face him. Reaching around the small of my back, I made to draw the compact Ruger from my waist.

It was gone. A smug grin pulled at his lips as he lifted his hand to show me the weapon in his hand.

Damn it.

The crowd shifted and bubbled around us, and we were shoved together once again. He grabbed onto the front of my shirt, and I felt his fingers barely skim my breasts under my V-neck.

Double gross.

"Hey! What the fuck is going on out there!?" a deep, commanding voice boomed from the stage. Guitars squealed as the music abruptly stopped.

The mass of bodies stopped moving as a thousand people looked around to see what was going on. As people around us started to back away, I took my opportunity to put some distance between the target and myself, but he held fast to my arm, crushing it in his grip. I countered, moving closer to shove my knee into his unguarded testicles. The crowd around us erupted in applause.

Did he release me from his vice-like grip? Yes, but not before planting *my* gun in the side of *my* face.

Asshole.

My knees buckled as stars formed behind my eyes, and I felt someone catch me as I sank to the floor.

"Hey! Buddy!" The thunderous voice yelled, "No is a complete sentence. Where the fuck is security? I think she needs help..."

Thirty minutes later, I sat on a gurney toward the back of a make-shift medic tent. I held an ice pack to my left cheek as Trent "Fox" Brooks, my teammate, stood next to me, laughing.

"You got your ass handed to you with your own gun," he chortled.

I glared up at him, "Oh, laugh it up. By the way...some wingman you are."

Throwing his hands up, he smiled, "As soon as I knew you couldn't hear me, I headed your way. I can't help that it was all over by the time I arrived."

Fox laughed again. He knew that if he poked fun at the entire incident, I wouldn't beat myself up about it. I've always been my own worst critic.

"Look, there were variables we couldn't control, we knew that. But we did the job. LEOs have the bad guy, and the girl is safe." He shrugged, "Take the win."

A security guard, a skinny, pimply faced kid that couldn't have been more than twenty-one, stepped around the privacy curtain, "Ma'am?"

My eyes shot in his direction.

"Mr. Johns would like to know if he could speak to you," I watched his Adam's apple bob in his long, thin neck as he swallowed nervously.

"Who?" I asked as a disembodied hand came to rest on the kid's bony shoulder.

"It's okay, Davey...I can handle it," a husky voice replied, and the kid disappeared back into the room. In his place stood a man with wide shoulders, a broad chest, sandy undercut hair, and sultry chocolate eyes. His black sleeveless shirt revealed well-muscled arms covered in a rainbow of tattoos. I immediately recognized him as the Obliterate lead singer.

"I'm sorry for intruding, I just wanted to make sure you were okay," he asked cautiously. "How's the head?"

Our eyes locked for a long moment before he spoke again, "That was a hell of a headbutt you gave him."

"You saw that?" I raised my brow.

"Yeah, you see a lot of things from where I am."

Well, that seemed a little arrogant.

"I'm Ioan Johns," he held his hand out for me to shake. I didn't.

Adjusting the icepack on my face, I smirked painfully, "Your name is John Johns?"

Ioan's eyes widened as his mouth opened once, then closed before it opened again to speak, "Yeah, how did you know that?"

"I know a little bit about a lot of things," I shrugged, then glanced at Fox. "Can we get out of here?"

Ioan touched the toe of my boot, speaking in a soothing tone, "Hey...that was a pretty good hit...maybe you could take a beat. Besides, the cops took that idiot out; he's not going to bother you in here."

I stared at him again. I wasn't sure who this guy thought he was, but I didn't need a savior, and I didn't need him to assure me I was safe. Throwing my legs over the edge of the bed, I tossed the ice pack on the thin mattress. The singer's eyes locked with mine again as I reached my hand out to Fox, and he placed my small Ruger in my palm. I holstered it behind my back and took sheer delight as Ioan's eyes widened.

"Nice meeting you," I said in passing as Fox and I made our exit into the starry night.

Prologue-Ioan

Rocking back in the overstuffed chair, I stared into the dark, watching street lamps and fast-food signs just off the interstate blur by as our tour bus raced to the next city. She walked out of the room without so much as a second glance. I closed my eyes, concentrating on the sound of her voice and the scent of her soft perfume.

"Hey!" Ezra punched my shoulder. "Asleep already?"

Jolting, my eyes popped open and I swiveled in the chair, looking up at him, "No, no...too wired for that."

"Same," he plopped in the matching chair, facing me. "Where are the guys?"

I bobbed my head toward the back of the bus, "Tomas is on the phone with Nina. I think Billy is already in the bunk."

"Yeah, I just talked to Val. Sounds like Sawyer is sick...ear infection," Leaning forward, Ezra slid open the storage just under the table, pulling out a deck of cards. Tipping them at me, his eyebrows arched.

I nodded, "Deal me in."

Ezra shuffled the deck before dealing us a game of Gin. I couldn't recount the hours we spent traveling and using this same deck as a time waster. Picking up my hand, I adjusted the cards, sorting into suits from lowest to highest.

"Did you ever find out what the fuck that was tonight? I wonder if that chick is okay," he flipped a card from the deck face up.

"I went to see her." Her green-streaked hazel eyes flashed in my mind.

Ezra chuckled, "No shit? Did she know that guy?"

Shaking my head, I made a discard, "I don't think so. Ez, she was carrying a gun."

"How'd she get in with that?" his eyes widened with shock.

I couldn't look him at him and I dropped my eyes back to the cards in my hand, "I don't know...I think maybe she's a cop."

Feeling my best friend's stare on me, I shifted in my seat, furrowing my brow to *really* concentrate.

"Ioan?" he pulled on my name.

Looking up, I tried to portray innocence, "Yeah?"

As if I could.

"What's going on?" he tossed his hand face down on the table. "You've got that look."

The corner of my mouth wrinkled, "What are you talking about? Dude, play your hand."

There was no way I was getting out of this. I wasn't sure how I slipped up, but somehow, Ezra could read it. How could I tell him that I just left the woman of my dreams behind?

"You got her number, didn't you?" Picking up his cards, he laughed gregariously.

It was at that moment, I broke. "Goddamn it! I wish."

"What stopped you? You said you went to see her." He glanced up from his cards, "Oh, God...her boyfriend slash husband was with her?"

"They didn't act like they were in a relationship, at least not a couple," I admitted. "More like, partners...I think."

Ezra crossed his arms, "Okay...not a husband."

"Ez, she blew me off. Like...she had zero interest in me. None." I explained, my excitement growing. "And it was the sexiest thing any woman has ever done."

His head tilted as if he was trying to understand what I said. I knew it was confusing. Just hearing the words come from my mouth, I heard how insane it sounded, but it didn't make it any less true.

"So, let me get this straight...this chick, gets into a fight with some guy she doesn't know and he knocks her senseless and she ends up in the infirmary. You go to see her and she shuts you down before you can even say hello...and that's sexy to you?" He snickered, "Dude, that's fucked up."

I shook my head, "Ez...it wasn't that she wasn't interested in me...she wasn't impressed at all. She treated me like any other person. How often does that happen to us?"

"From someone on the outside? Never." he agreed.

"Right! And God, man...she's gorgeous. That's the kind of woman I want. Someone...normal. Down to Earth, you know? Not someone who thinks only about what I can do for them." I could have continued with my fantasizing about her, but I thought it might get weird.

"So, she's cute?" he thumbed over his cards.

I groaned, "Long brown hair...tall-ish. These hazel eyes that flash with green fire...and a body that's all real, you know? What I wouldn't give to have my hands on those hips of hers. Damn, she's beautiful."

Ezra bobbed his head, holding back a larger laugh, "I got it. The opposite of Tessie."

"Seriously?" My eyes rolled, chuckling. "You're never going to let me live her down, are you?"

"My best friend in the world dating a self-centered, obnoxious, shallow, couldn't-find-a-developing country-on-a-map-if-you-paid-her heiress whose only goal in life was to be worshiped by everyone on the planet? Not a chance in hell." His laughter carried throughout the cabin.

I may have deserved that.

"I'll hand it to you, this girl, whoever she is, can definitely take care of herself. Put that in the pro column." He continued. "I bet someone knows her name…maybe you should look her up?"

I thought about that as well. It wasn't just her looks that attracted me to her. She had a presence that quietly commanded respect. I didn't think she would appreciate someone, anyone, chasing her down.

"Nah, I don't think so. Besides, it's a fleeting moment, right? And, I'm not a creep," I kicked back further into my chair.

"Yeah, I'd hate for your face to look like that guys' tonight," He paused, lying his fanned cards down in front of him, "By the way, Gin. I win."

Chapter One

Alyssa

I want it to be fully known that I, Alyssa Salerno, unequivocally, and without shame or apology, hate Las Vegas.

It's loud, crowded, and bright. They call New York the city that never sleeps; well, neither does Vegas. I despise the desert, I loathe tourists, and the amount of money that flows through this city of nearly seven hundred thousand could feed a third-world nation. But what I hate most of all is the heat.

"But it's a dry heat."

No, it's the oppressive fever of summer that bears down on your person like it's trying to consume your soul, and it is the absolute last thing I want to contend with on a daily basis. Especially at five o'clock in the morning.

But here I am. In Las Vegas. My current hometown.

My cursing of the summer heat was interrupted as my cell phone buzzed in my pocket. Realizing it was only Fox, I let it go to voicemail as I pulled open the heavy glass door of Onyx Industries corporate office. Icy air hit my face as the tiny droplets of sweat that built on my temples in just the short half-block walk from the coffee shop immediately dried. I noticed Fox, black tactical pants and shirt, not one strand of his sandy-blonde hair out of place, standing at the bank of elevators staring at his phone, and I knew he was debating whether to call me back or not.

"I'm gone ten minutes..." I stopped at his side.

"Fifteen," he countered, his crystalline blue eyes sparkling with delight. He was always ready with a smart ass barb.

I scoffed, "It's bad enough that I'm being forced to be up at five am...don't time me before I've had caffeine."

Fox lifted his travel mug at me, "Come prepared next time."

The elevator dinged, and we stepped inside.

"I forgot you were a Boy Scout," I lifted my cup to my lips and took a giant swig of the dark, cold brew.

"Eagle scout, actually."

I rolled my eyes, "Whatever."

Fox sipped from his mug, "Any idea why the early morning call? Some diplomat get caught ankle deep in hookers again?"

"No idea," I laughed lightly, remembering the incident three years ago. "I was about to ask you the same question."

We rode in silence to the tenth floor, me, taking long pulls from my cup as the dinging of the elevator at each floor lulled me into a daydream of lying in my bed just a couple of hours ago. It was at the ungodly hour of three-thirty this morning when our handler's name came over on my phone.

"Wheels," I answered sleepily, calling him by my term of endearment. Jake Merritt, was a former Army Ranger, Purple Heart recipient, paraplegic, and a man who could take a joke. It was during a small spat when we first met that I blurted out some sort of curse and insult that ended with me granting him the moniker.

He laughed until I thought he might pass out, then told me I had some of the biggest balls he'd ever seen.

"Lys...we've had a job come to us on short notice overnight. I need you and your team here zero-five-thirty," he stated in a way that told me he was clearly way more awake than I was. Which meant he was caffeinated, and I was jealous.

Rubbing my eyes, I tossed the blanket off my legs, "Yeah...I mean, I know Fox is still available. Chico too. I'm not sure whether Bett has made it back from Oregon or not."

"Bett is here. She's already into a threat analysis," he said.

I contemplated my next words. It wasn't as though a middle-of-the-night phone call was all that unusual, but considering I only walked into my apartment six hours earlier from a trans-Atlantic flight from Paris, where I spent the entire time playing bodyguard to an ambassador's mother-in-law, I thought I would have at least a day to myself. And honestly, it was more like babysitting. After her third Gin Gimlet, the mother-in-law had a hard time keeping her hands off the male flight attendant's ass.

And I hadn't even cuddled Daisy yet.

"I appreciate the work, Jake," I yawned, "But isn't there..."

"No, Lys. I need you on this job."

The elevator's last bell brought me back to reality. Fox made a grand gesture with his arm, "After you."

I rolled my eyes, "Huh. So, that's what it takes for you to be a gentleman? Early morning wake-up call?"

Fox was still laughing as he pulled the large oak door to the conference room open. Jake sat in his chair at the head of the table, Bett, our team analyst, just to his right. Her short, fire engine red bob looked a little disheveled along with her black pencil skirt and white Oxford shirt. I noticed two empty cups in her general space, telling me she probably hadn't been to sleep since her red-eye back to Vegas.

Next to her was Chico. He just barely pushed six feet, but he was broad across the shoulders and had a stare that would make a priest shiver. He reminded me of a younger and better-looking Danny Trejo, mustache and all. In reality? The most loyal teddy bear around.

To Jake's left sat a well-built man of around thirty-five. I didn't recognize him, so I could only assume it was our new client. He didn't have the look of one of our typical emergencies; those were usually ones that smelled of old, generational wealth and power. Not this guy. He looked like the handsome extra from a music video.

"Ezra Stanley, let me introduce you," Jake didn't hesitate with the getting-to-know-you portion of the morning. "Alyssa Salerno and Fox Brooks. They'll be leading the operation and will serve as the points of contact."

I took a seat next to Chico, "What can we do for you, Mr. Stanley?"

The man's eyes were kind, and he had an all-American look to him; or he would have if it wasn't for the two facial piercings, wide hoops in his ears, and long, black hair pulled back into a neat ponytail. I spied a scrolling tattoo peeking out of the top of his buttoned shirt collar as well.

"Mr. Stanley is part of a very well-known rock band and is offering support to another member who will be along shortly. It seems as though this group's lead vocalist has somewhat of a stalker," Jake explained. "Bett, can you fill us in with the details while we're waiting?"

"Absolutely," her southern drawl coated our ears like warm honey. "It seems our girl is quite smart. None of the letters contain any fingerprints or saliva, so she's worn gloves throughout the whole process. Emails are the same...on the surface, virtually untraceable, but we're gonna keep working on those. There have been gifts of one sort or another, phone calls even after numbers have been changed..."

"What's in the letters, Bett?" Chico drew his hand down his dark mustache.

"Oh," she flipped open the thick folder on the table in front of her and passed out samples. "They started five months ago...your basic fan mail sort of thing. Then we have examples of some escalation. *I love you with all my soul...we're meant to be...we can spend eternity together.* You know...the crazy is starting to show."

Glancing up from my document, my eyes met Mr. Stanley's, "When did the switch flip?"

"Two weeks ago," I watched as he twirled his wedding band on his left hand. "Courier brought a gift to a show. Turned out to be a dead rat."

"That'll do it," Fox's head bobbed as Chico pulled a hiss through his teeth.

I thrust my chin at Jake, "What's the plan? We shadow this guy? See if stalker-girl pokes her head out?"

"No," he shook his head. "We've got to be a little more calculating. Whoever this person is, she's smart...and with a disposable income. The rat showed up in Minneapolis, followed by another hand-delivered letter in Chicago two days later. We're going to need to go deep. I've had Bett set you up with a full cover...all the bells and whistles."

"Cover? For what, exactly?" I prodded. I was getting the feeling I wasn't going to like this plan.

"We need someone to be at his side twenty-four, seven. Lys, your new *boyfriend* is a bona fide rockstar."

Chapter Two

Alyssa

Mr. Stanley's phone buzzed, and he immediately rose from the table to answer. While he walked away to a corner, I turned on Jake.

"Are you kidding me? Is this the plan? What's my story, huh?" I hissed. "What about Fox? Or Chico? One of them could easily be a bodyguard. And what am I going to do at home? I just got back and Dai—"

"I took care of everything," Bett assured me. "The stalker can run your name through a Google search all she wants and find that Lyssie Blackwell started modeling at sixteen before taking a hiatus at twenty to pursue her art degree. After that, she worked as an actress in London for a few years before returning to the US."

I looked at my analyst in complete shock. Model? She had to be kidding. And I couldn't draw a stick figure to save my hell-bound soul. But before I could ask another question or even voice a protest, Stanley was back.

"He's on his way."

Leaning over, Fox whispered in my ear, "Oooo, this better be good. What do you think? Are we looking at a Mick Jagger? Lys, you like older men, right?"

"Eat shit, asshole." I ground my teeth and fought back the urge to smack the bottom of his cup and watch him spill his coffee all over his neatly pressed tactical shirt.

He was still laughing when the door swung open to reveal a well-built man in a black suit and tie. He was clean-shaven, including the sandy undercut that once covered his head. The black plugs in both earlobes, combined with his intense brown eyes, lent to his overall intimidating appearance and was much different from the man who introduced himself to me a year ago. This man looked like a wealthy mob boss from one of my smutty romance novels.

Ioan Johns.

Meeting Johns at the doors threshold, Stanley motioned for him to take a seat. The man barely had enough time to get comfortable before his bandmate made introductions. Ioan's eyes immediately met mine, and the recognition was instant.

"It's you!" he exclaimed pointedly, and I smiled politely.

Jake's eyes bounced between the pair of us, "Do you two know each other?"

"Uhh, sir. Rinaldo op last year? Alyssa ran into her own gun?" Fox smirked. My eyes rolled as I turned to my partner, the anger on my face palpable. He always had a way of pissing me off in the most inopportune moments. Forget the coffee; he was lucky I didn't break his nose right there.

"Ah, yes," Jake nodded. "I remember now."

He turned to the men, "We had a last-minute client that we assisted at one of your shows last year. Alyssa here was instrumental in taking down a man known for trafficking young girls."

"Asshole," Stanley replied.

Turning his chair toward Ioan, Jake spoke directly to the man, "Mr. Johns...I understand that this situation has you a little rattled. We will get this person. As quickly as possible, so you can go about your life. We have a plan that will not only provide you with round-the-clock protection but will, hopefully, infuriate the person behind this so they make a mistake. That's when they'll be caught."

The weight of Ioan's eyes on me felt heavy. I wasn't sure if he was still putting the pieces of our first meeting together or if he took issue with the fact that I was a woman. Either way, I really didn't care. I just wanted him to stop staring at me.

Finally, he turned to Jake, "What exactly is your plan? As I'm sure Ezra told you, we're kind of going off-sides for this."

"Can you explain why that is?" Jake asked pointedly. "We're very accustomed to working with a management team and can do so here, if you prefer."

Ioan shook his head, "You have to understand, Mr. Merritt, while I'm sure you've heard the phrase *'Any press is good press'*, I don't believe that. While Siren means well, they would shoot this to the moon, as it were. Use it to their advantage. I'd rather keep them and our manager out of the loop here."

"Understood."

"I do have a concern," Ioan cleared his throat. "We have a security team already...and now, I'll have my own bodyguard?"

"No, that's too obvious. Mr. Stanley tells me you're single, yes?" Jake asked, and Ioan nodded. "We're using that as our point of entry. We're ready to set Alyssa up here as your girlfriend. Since you want to keep this out of your already established circle, we're also prepared to keep an eye on things from a distance. Bett," Jake nodded in her direction, "is ready to pull the trigger with your approval."

The man's eyes danced from Bett to Jake, "What does that mean?"

"Bett?" Jake nodded. Following his order, Bett took a thin remote from the conference table and pointed it over her head. The television screen glowed blue as she typed a few commands on her laptop, and her screen was cast for us all to see. News articles, social media posts, and pictures of Ioan and me flipped on the screen like a book page. No one could tell that they were completely fake.

"Uhhh...hello, Mr. Johns, big fan," she stammered, then paused. Ioan's lips parted into a cocky grin.

He's just as arrogant as the last time we met.

Bett continued, "As you can see, I've created an entire back story for you and Lys. With your say so, my program will hit all the necessary outlets confirming your dating status. It should only take a few hours for the information to really hit socials, and I suspect a couple of days to go viral. By that time, you both will be back in LA and ready to make public appearances."

"Won't that be obvious? I mean, it's hard to keep any secret in the industry these days...this...stalker, or whatever...she knows everything about me. Won't it be a little weird when I suddenly have a live-in partner?" he replied.

"No. Actually, it won't," I stated flatly. I didn't like this plan any more than he did, but Bett was the absolute best in the business, and I wasn't going to let him think otherwise.

Crossing his large arms over his chest, he frowned, "Why is that?"

"There are plenty of examples where celebrities have kept their private lives...private," I crossed my arms over my chest. Two could play that game.

"Huh," he scoffed, but I didn't let him continue.

"When did you first hear of Reeves-Grant? Or Swift-Alwyn? Those relationships were going on for years before the public knew. It's a solid plan," I nodded my approval at Bett, who stared at me, eyes wide and jaw dropped, from around Chico's shoulder.

He considered me for a long moment. Never taking his eyes off mine, he spoke to his friend, "What'd you think Ez? You good with this?"

"I am."

Ioan Johns let out a sigh. "Alright, let's catch this woman."

Chapter Three

Ioan

Twenty-four hours later, we were on a plane.

Forty thousand feet in the air and an hour and twenty minutes isn't nearly enough time to get to know your new girlfriend. If we were going to be stuck together for the next however long it took to catch this stalker, we would have to be civil to one another. She clearly didn't like me, and I wasn't sure at exactly what point that happened.

She seemed to ignore me for the first third of the flight, using the awkward silence to read on her tablet. Afterward, she stared out the window of the private plane, her fingernails tapping in rhythm on the table between us. I know I shouldn't be staring, but she *was* beautiful and I kept thinking back to our first encounter.

She was dismissive of me and really flippant. Looking back, I understood; it was a job, and that was all, and getting hurt seemed to be part of the territory. But it was the way she couldn't have cared less about who I was, if she tried. She didn't want anything from me, and she certainly wasn't going to pretend that she did.

It was the sexiest move I'd ever witnessed, and from that night a year ago, I knew that was the kind of woman I wanted in my life. I couldn't help but stare as the sun glinted off her brunette and caramel-streaked hair, and I watched her hazel-green eyes gaze out the window.

Clearing my throat, I offered her something to drink, "Do you want a beer...or something?"

An intense stare moved in my direction, "Thank you, but I don't drink."

She looked back at the window. This was going to be harder than I thought.

"We have water...or what about a soda?"

She shook her head.

I had to go for broke. I knew we were being forced into this situation, but the least we could do was be civil with each other. She seemed to have a grudge against me already and for absolutely no reason. I was having a hard time believing her acting skills were going to be stellar, and that this charade would fall apart before it got started.

Leaning on the table separating us, I crossed my arms over it, "Look, I have the feeling that you aren't exactly pleased with this job. And you're not exactly my biggest fan. Though...I don't know why—"

Her eyeroll broke my sentence.

"What?" I asked.

Man, this woman was relentless.

"I understand that you want to make nice or whatever this is, but Mr. Johns, this is my job. I am more than happy to take care of myself and my own needs. There's no need for you and me to be friends outside of the public eye," she replied curtly, and it kind of hurt.

"Ioan," I offered.

Her sharp eyes cut back to mine, "What?"

"Mr. Johns sounds like my father is standing behind me," I laughed. To my utter surprise, a glint of a grin pulled at her lips, and her face transformed, like magic. She was beautiful in her all-business, stern exterior, but even that hint of a smile radiated something angelic. Just as quickly as it appeared, the soft smile faded, and she held her hand out to me.

"You can call me Alyssa," she said. "Or, Lys, if you prefer."

Taking her small hand in mine, I found it not to be as delicate as it looked. Her grip was just as strong as mine, and the silky top side of her hand was a stark contrast to the calluses I felt in her palm.

"We will be arriving in Van Nuys in twenty minutes." The pilot's speaker crackled as he put it back on its base.

Alyssa rose from her seat. "That's my cue."

It wasn't until the pilot made his announcement for the final descent into the small airport that she reappeared from the bathroom, and her transformation was a complete one-eighty. Changing out of her designer black suit and heels, she wore tight jeans, a loose button-up shirt, and ankle boots. Her tight ponytail was replaced with loose waves that hung just past her shoulders, and she added a darker shade of lipstick than she wore earlier.

She tossed her aviators on the table between us. "Our play begins as soon as we deplane."

Snapping her seatbelt, she pulled it tighter. "This is more than fake it until we make it. We have to immediately be a couple. It has to be believable or she'll never buy it...Have you ever done improv?" her brow raised. I swallowed hard and hoped she wouldn't notice.

My throat was so dry. We were jumping right into the deep end. No rehearsal or life preserver.

"Uhh...I mean, I am a musician," I tried to sound confident, but I knew it came off as cocky.

Her eyes rolled again, "Then you know it's about teamwork. You have to be just as attentive to what I say and my body language as I am to yours...the first few times it will feel awkward. But, the more we practice, the easier it will be."

"How many times have you done this?" I asked, curious about exactly the kind of security work Onyx Industries actually did.

"A few."

Raising my brows in an attempt to solicit a deeper conversation, she instead ignored me.

"We will also need a code if we're ever separated and there's trouble," Alyssa continued. "But we can come up with that later."

The plane's wheels skipped and screeched on the tarmac, and within a few minutes, we were taxiing to our designated parking spot near the terminal. This morning, I wasn't confident about Onyx's plan at all, and to be honest, I still wasn't. But this was the best solution for now. I'm not usually worried about fans; on the contrary, most of them are perfectly sane, level-headed, nice people who understand the meaning of privacy. I just couldn't imagine what went wrong with this one.

Part of me wanted to empathize with...whoever they were. What kind of trauma in their life drove them to such madness as fixating on me? Were they just lonely? Or maybe they saw themselves in me? For the most part, I've been open about certain parts of my life and my struggles. I wondered if they were going through something similar and, for whatever reason, this was how they chose to ask for help.

The familiar smell of industrial cleaner and paint assaulted my nostrils as the cool air from the terminal swept over us as we walked inside. She adjusted her large handbag over her shoulder and slipped her hand into mine. For a quick moment, I forgot about the plan as she wove her fingers loosely with mine.

"Ioan! Ioan! Over here!" a voice said over a small group of three men with cameras.

Goddamn paparazzi. Flashes snapped in our faces as the group stepped in our way, demanding attention and time.

"Ioan...is this the girlfriend you've been hiding? What's her name?" one asked as a cell phone, I'm sure was recording, was shoved in our faces.

Another cell phone came out of nowhere, and a rogue hand pushed into Lys' shoulder, shoving her into me. Before I could growl an obscenity, Fox came from nowhere, stepping between us and them.

"Car is waiting just outside," he called over his shoulder.

"When did you get here?" Alyssa asked as I pulled her along next to me.

Fox continued to block the photographers, "Yesterday. Why am I always the one on time?"

Once far enough away that we knew we weren't being followed, I slowed our pace to a more casual one, allowing her to catch her breath. Within minutes, the warm SoCal sun was overhead, and we were putting baggage in the back of our ride.

"I thought your girl was sure this wouldn't go public until at least tomorrow," I growled, sliding into the back of the black Suburban.

Alyssa shrugged, "A few idiots with cameras don't make a viral moment. I'll give you credit, though...you did a good job in there. You didn't flinch when I took your hand."

I felt my face flush, and I prayed she wouldn't notice.

The drive to my house in Santa Monica was silent. It wasn't until we made the final turn onto Georgina Avenue that I really noticed my surroundings. The car pulled up to the gate, and the driver punched in his code before we came to a stop on the other side. Marco Gatti, our band's manager, met us in the breezeway between my courtyard and the pool.

"I'm so glad you made it!" he said, a touch of concern in his voice. "Any trouble?"

"No. All good," I replied immediately. "Marco, this is Lyssie Blackwell. The woman I told you about."

"The woman you've been hiding," He held out a stubby hand as his dark, beady eyes narrowed on her to a point that his cheeks nearly buried them as they rose. "Blackwell? You look Italian."

"I am, on my mother's side," she lied politely, as her Italian heritage actually came from her father; that much was clear with a surname like Salerno.

I saw she recognized Marco's thick New York accent, and it confirmed to her that he definitely was as well, and as a matter of fact, he was just a generation or two out of the Old Country. And that was set-ting aside the fact that Marco was the stereotype, diamond-encrusted pinky ring and all.

He slapped me on the shoulder, "Fantastic. So, I'll get out of your hair and you two can settle in. Ioan, call me tomorrow. We've got to get the rest of the recording schedule confirmed with the guys for this new album."

I nodded, and he left. I drew a deep breath, thankful to be home, when a small prickle on the back of my neck drew my attention. Turning in her direction, I found her staring at me. Her eyes seemed to cut into my flesh like jeweled daggers. I wondered what she was thinking. I wanted to ask, but I was sure she wouldn't tell me anyway.

"Question. How did he get in here?" she asked.

Her question took me by surprise, "Marco? He has his own code. Why?"

She pursed her lips, and it was then that I realized how perfectly plump they were, even if the look she gave me seemed almost danger-ous.

"I'm going to need to know everyone that comes and goes with their own code," she drew a deep breath, then let it out slowly. "Everyone. Even the pizza delivery kid."

The brow over her left eye arched with an unspoken question. It was as if she were saying, *Do you understand?*

"Yeah, of course," I rubbed my hand over my head. "So, I guess...I should show you around."

Chapter Four

Alyssa

I reached for my suitcase, and so did Ioan. Wrinkling my nose at the indiscretion, I waited for him to let go, but it seemed we were in a standoff.

"I can carry my own bag," I said flatly, and he looked at me in the same manner.

"I get that, but aren't we supposed to be *dating*? What if she's watching?" he made another move for the case.

We're only a few hours in, and this guy is driving me nuts.

"Whoever is stalking you isn't watching you right now," I took the handle of my bag. "So, no need to play bellboy."

Scooping my luggage away, I turned into a covered area that turned out to be an outdoor kitchen. Accepting his fate, Ioan rushed ahead of me to open the door. I nodded my appreciation, pulling my bag over the threshold.

Ioan's mansion wasn't really a mansion at all, at least not by the entertainment industry standards. Set back on a regular street behind a concrete privacy wall and iron gate in the North of Montana neighborhood, his three-bedroom was expansive, but not what I would consider extravagant and not at all pretentious.

The three-story edifice featured entire walls of glass on the back side of the house and some nice amenities. A weight room, pool, and outdoor kitchen on the ground level. Three bedrooms, three of the four bathrooms upstairs, and a music room with recording booth and modest theater on the lower level. The home was decorated cleanly with neutral colors and dark wood accents; nothing to indicate this was the home of a Grammy-winning world-touring rock star.

At least, it's not what I expected.

Over the years, I worked with some of the most elitist humans on the planet. The type of people who wouldn't call you by name because to do so would raise you to the level of equal. New money trash who thought drinking Dom Perignon for breakfast was luxury and old money assholes who refused to tip more than fifty cents for a one-hundred dollar meal.

None of them would be caught dead in this house. Was it huge? Yes. Did it have a few frivolous amenities? Also yes. But, considering the alternative, this home was surprisingly normal.

"I'll take you upstairs," Ioan offered, reaching out for my suitcase again. He saw my reaction and immediately dropped his hand. "Sorry...forgot, you don't like men helping."

"I never said that!" I barked.

A wrinkle formed between his eyes. "So, you like men?"

"I do...do you?" snapping back my retort and instantly regretting it.

Reading up on Ioan Johns on the plane, I knew the speculation surrounding him and his personal life. Never discussing family or a significant other put the press into a tailspin, and rumor mills pumped out whispers and gossip sold as truth. And this had been going on for years, even though he did, in fact, have some very beautiful and very famous exes.

I honestly didn't care if he was straight, gay, bi, or had an affinity for a Martian; I just wanted to do my job.

"Exactly what are you insinuating? Just because my house isn't filled with naked models and lines of cocaine, I must not be attracted to women? I mean, what kind of rock-and-roll guy am I?!" his words seemed more filled with hurt than rage.

I knew I'd crossed a line. I had to de-escalate this, or Jake would most likely fire me—if Ioan fired us.

Stepping off the first riser of the stairs, I smiled softly, "A man with a very nice home."

Ioan drew a deep breath, letting it out slowly, and I removed my hand from my baggage as a peace offering. He took it, proceeding up the stairs ahead of me. After reaching the landing, we walked down the entire length of the hallway, where he opened the last door on the right.

"My master suite is the door on the left as you come up the stairs. I thought you'd be comfortable here...but, all the rooms have private bathrooms...if you'd rather have something else," his voice trailed off as his soulful eyes locked on mine.

I shook my head, "No, this is just fine."

"Good," his smile returned. "I'll leave you to it. If you need anything, I'll be in my room...the blinds are on timers, so make sure you leave a light on if you leave, and please help yourself to anything in the kitchen."

Awesome. The backside of this house was mostly windows, and automated blinds would make it nice and dark in here.

Awesome.

"Thank you," I swallowed hard, my throat immediately desert-like.

Ioan nodded, turned, and left the room.

Chapter Five

Ioan

"**M**an, I don't know about this," I kicked my shoes off into my closet, an Air pod wedged into my ear canal. Sitting on the edge of my bed, I stared out at the street just beyond the rock wall that defined my property. I heard ice rattling and Ezra swallowed before he replied.

"Yo, Onyx came highly recommended, remember? We've got to get this crazy bitch off your back," he paused. "Off *our* backs. Do you really want to go back on tour looking over your shoulder all the time?"

"No," my eyes rolled to the ceiling, "But, this woman they've hooked me up with...she's like steel."

"I still can't believe she's the same chick you drooled over last year," he laughed. I heard high pitched squeals, a thud, and the cry of a child. "Seriously, Summit?! Put that bat down and apologize to your brother!"

The normality of that comment made me smile.

Ezra continued, "I thought that whole cold thing is what you liked about her."

He wasn't wrong. When I met Alyssa a year ago in the infirmary, after she head butted some asshole that assaulted her at one of our shows, I talked about her for weeks. Well, not *her* exactly, but her demeanor, her flippant personality, the sense I got that she wasn't impressed by me in the least. I knew I was a decent looking guy and I took care of myself, so having a woman completely blow me off was special and a surprising new turn-on.

I swore if I ever had the opportunity to meet another woman like that, I wouldn't allow her to disappear into the ether. I wanted, or, rather needed, someone like her in my life. Someone that I could just be Ioan Johns, the quiet-night-at-home-with-a-book-cheesy-action-movie-watching-nerd with and not just Ioan Johns, the rockstar. I had fanciful daydreams about falling in love and maybe even marriage.

"It is," I replied, swearing under my breath.

"Then what's the problem?" Ezra crunched on ice. "Dude, she's gorgeous and again...that ice queen thing."

"Maybe the fantasy is easier than the reality? Besides, this woman for sure does not like me. I'm only a job, that much is clear. Being dismissive of this presumed social status is one thing, but, I'm fairly certain Ms. Salerno hates me," I mused.

"Ooo, Ms. Salerno. Sounds like a teacher kink," he laughed.

I let out an exhaustive sigh right before Ezra's tone changed, "Sean! Just because your little brother hit you does not mean you hit him back!" A pause then, "Sean, we are not debating this. Either put the bat back or take a nap...those are your choices."

The clatter in the background told me that my nephew made the correct choice.

"Sorry, man," he returned his attention to our call. "Look, Yo...she's right in that regard, you are her job right now. I know you've got it bad for her, I saw it the second you recognized her the other day in the office—"

"No, I don't," I protested. A thought occurred to me and I wondered if my long-time best friend had been playing matchmaker. "Ez, did you know she worked for Onyx Industries before we hired them?"

Laughter roared from his chest, "Man, shut the fuck up. Who are you trying to play with? I've known you too goddamn long for all that. Just let her do what you're paying her to do and if shit happens, it happens." He paused, "And no, I had no idea. They just came highly recommended."

God, I hated when this asshole was right, so I changed the subject, "Marco was here waiting when we pulled up."

"Oh, perfect. He harassing you about the schedule confirmation or being nosy about your girlfriend?" He crunched on more ice.

I stripped off my jeans, tossing them into the hamper, and pulled on basketball shorts, "A little of both. I think more on the nosy side. Alyssa wasn't impressed."

"Ah, Marco is harmless. He was nice to her, right?"

Crossing the room, I sat in my high back chair and picked up my copy of *Return of the King.* Running my thumb over the edges of the pages I replied, "I think he was a little smitten with her, honestly. Her being Italian and all."

Another roar of laughter, "God, imagine if you have to fight Marco for your girl."

I didn't want to. One, because years ago, all of us in the band, Ezra, Billy, Tomas, and I, decided Marco was most definitely mob adjacent and none of us were going to mess with that. And two, she wasn't my girl. Not yet, if ever.

Soon, Ez and I said our goodbyes and disconnected our call. Propping my legs on the ottoman, I flicked on the lamp next to me and cracked my book open. I sat in the chair for more than an hour attempting to thwart the dark forces of Sauron to no avail. Deciding to come back later when my head was a little less filled with nonsense, I left the room in search of food.

Coming around the corner of the open kitchen, I pulled on the refrigerator door. After realizing my dinner would have to come from the freezer instead, I grabbed a bottle of sparking water before circling back to the pantry and a soft giggle caught me off guard. Poking my head back around the corner, I looked for the source of the sound, when it happened again.

Was someone else in my house? I never heard Alyssa leave her room and I immediately thought of my need for Onyx Industries in the first place.

Shit.

Moving stealthily through the kitchen, I held the unopened, glass bottle of water to my side, ready to defend myself if necessary. I knew the stalker had my address. After we came off tour a few months ago, the same creepy letters started showing up here as well as a dead snake on my gate.

I didn't want to hurt anyone, but I would if I had too.

I worked my way through the living room and my office, before hearing Alyssa's voice just beyond my home gym. I stopped in the doorway when I heard the laughter for a third time.

Two of the four walls of the gym were floor to ceiling windows facing the breezeway leading to my back patio. Landscaped with large greenery, it provided, what I thought, was a beautiful entrance to my personal oasis in the back. Alyssa stood among the palms and Ficus smiling and chatting away expressively.

That smile was beautiful and infectious and I caught my lips pulling at their edges just seeing it. Whomever she was talking to was the luckiest person on earth, because to receive an expression like that? That was all adoration and love.

Popping the lid on my bottle, I turned away from the door and returned to the freezer pilfering. I nuked some chicken curry and carried it, my bottle of water, and a bowl of fruit up the stairs and back to my room. Settling back into my chair and ottoman, I flipped on the television to find my evening plans set with a little help from Lethal Weapon's Sergeant Murtaugh.

Chapter Six

Alyssa

As expected, my night was restless, but I managed to get a few hours of sleep and a quick shower before emerging from my room a little after six am. I was actually quite excited to be back in LA. It's not nearly as hot as Vegas, and as long as I avoided the common tourist traps like the Walk of Fame, I'd negate a couple of the things I hated back home. Also, it seemed Ioan Johns lived six blocks from a public beach; it could be worse.

After an early call to Bett about the virility of mine and Ioan's leaked relationship status, I tipped the older gentleman who brought my coffee delivery and settled onto one of the outdoor sofas near the pool.

One of the requests I made to Bett was an all-access mirror from Ioan's calendar to mine. I wanted to get a feel for exactly how strictly his schedule was maintained and followed. If he lived and died by his agenda, then I'd have to reasonably assume this could be an inside job. However, if he was more inclined to go about his day with little structure, there would be more opportunity for a stranger stalking. Anyone watching for a long period of time could learn his movements and routines, no matter how small.

I sipped my cold brew and thumbed through the past three months of activity. Most of his time was on tour, which was incredibly dependent on timeliness, even down to what time the band would be fed. Unfortunately, a good number of the timetables would be mostly public or at least known to no less than one hundred people or more.

It wasn't that helpful.

I went back further, if for no other reason than to compare year after year. It was here I saw a pattern emerge. After going back three years, all the data we requested, I saw that every two months or so, Ioan had two, sometimes three days blocked out as *Personal*. Then in July of last year, a month after our first meeting, the *personal* days stopped appearing.

I made a mental note to ask Bett to check into it.

Fast-forwarding to his current calendar, I noticed today was going to be busy. Ioan had to complete two radio interviews and one with *Rolling Stone*. The rest of his day looked clear, but I remembered Marco mentioning a phone call to discuss the recording schedule. Looking ahead a few days, I noticed several blocks of time where he would be at a place called Neptune's Noodle. A quick Google search told me it was a recording studio in Hollywood.

Damn it. I knew this job was too good to be true. Hollywood definitely wasn't on my top-ten-places-to-be list.

Flipping my screen, I resumed the research I started on the plane the day before. If I wanted to catch this person, I had to find out what they knew, which meant I needed to read everything I could about Obliterate and Ioan Johns. Going back to the beginning, I found fifteen-year-old video clips of the band performing second stage at large festivals and opening for much larger and well-known groups at the time. There were Grammy wins and performances. Video magazine interviews. Countless YouTube pieces shot from someone in the audience of a show and archives of lyrics; those I bookmarked for later.

As I opened up one of the archival sites, I heard the rustle of footsteps coming near. Raising my eyes, I watched Ioan in a t-shirt and flannel lounge pants, walking in my direction with two fresh cups of coffee.

He set one of the mugs next to me. "Good morning."

I looked from the mug then back to Ioan before tipping my delivered beverage to my lips. "Good morning."

"You got Little Bean," he smiled, taking a pull from his cup. "Eddie deliver it?"

I glanced over my drink, "Skinny, older man...greying around the edges?"

Ioan smiled, "That's him. Cool guy...used to be a tour guide at the Museum of Natural History."

Sitting back, I considered him for a moment. I wouldn't have expected someone of his caliber to take an interest in an old man delivering coffee. I weighed the possibility he could be making it up to endear himself to me, or...he could be telling the truth. I returned to looking at my tablet and moved back to the calendar.

"It looks like you've got a pretty busy day," I reported.

Ioan cocked his head. "Did someone share my calendar with you?"

"No," closing my tablet, I gathered my coffee and rose to leave. Ioan stared at me, waiting for an answer. I sighed reluctantly, "We're trying to catch someone who is at the least mentally unstable and at worst probably wants you dead. I have to know everything. Your calendar has been mirrored to mine. No one but Onyx and you know I have access."

He nodded, but I continued as if he were getting ready to interrupt. I heard these same arguments from countless clients before, and with very little sleep, I wasn't about to rehash the reasons why at length.

"I know...it's an invasion of privacy, but you need to understand that I'm...*we're* trying to keep you safe. If you can get behind that—"

"No," he stood, grabbing the coffee he sat on the table for me. "I'm completely fine with all of it. Let me know what else you need to know." He leaned toward me, "I've got nothing to hide."

He walked to the large, glass door before turning back, "My first interview is at nine...it's in the studio. You might want to get ready, Lyssie."

Chapter Seven

Ioan

At eight-fifteen, I pulled my navy Mercedes AMG Hybrid out of the garage and parked it in the front drive. I hated using a car service, and I was perfectly capable of driving myself and Alyssa to the satellite radio offices downtown. Certainly a milk run.

I just exited the car when I saw Alyssa pull the front door shut. I checked my phone to ensure the house was locked tight before meeting her at the side of the car to open the door. Her eyes squinted at me through her oversized sunglasses.

"Making this look real," I smiled broadly. She gave me a smirk of approval and slid onto the leather seat. Within a few minutes, we were buckled in, and I made a right onto my street heading for the ten.

"Nice car," she ran her fingers over the stitching of the seat.

"Yeah," I shrugged. "I prefer my Hellcat...but some of my neighbors think it's too loud."

As I glanced in her direction, I watched Lys' eyes widen, "You have a Hellcat? What year?"

"Nineteen sixty-eight," I chuckled. "Why?"

"Okay, that's pretty cool," she cut her eyes at me deviously.

I would never let her see it, but I was wholly impressed with her reaction. It wasn't every day that I was lucky enough to talk cars with a gorgeous woman.

"Would you want to take it out tonight? I got a text from Marco earlier...he wants to have dinner and go over some contract stuff," I glanced in her direction as I entered the freeway.

"Sounds like a date," she pulled out her phone and typed in a message. "Where is dinner? What time?"

I realized she was relaying the details to her team. Which, I understood, was all part of the procedure, but it was no less off-putting.

"Seven o'clock...Giraldi's over in Venice," I replied.

She typed away, "Perfect."

We drove for several miles in silence as she answered the numerous text messages that pinged on her phone. After a while, she leaned back in her seat and sighed. "Okay! We're all set for tonight...so, tell me, what should I expect at this interview?"

"It's pretty cut and dry...promotion for the new album," I replied.

She put her phone down. "I didn't think you'd recorded it yet."

"Well, not all of it, we've got three more songs to get down...which, the record company isn't really happy about that," I veered to the left, taking my exit.

"Why is that?"

I laughed, "Let's call it creative differences."

Out of the corner of my eye, I saw Alyssa turn in her seat to look at me straight on. "What does that mean?"

"It means," I chortled. "The guys and I know what our sound is and how it should evolve. Mikal disagrees."

"Mikal Stavopolos, the owner of your label?" she confirmed.

I made another turn, moving closer to our destination, "Mikal is pissed off we brought in another producer on this one...he wants some creative control. Even threatened to drop us." I laughed again, "He's a fucking punk...but we play nice around here. He knows other labels are lining up to work with us."

Rounding the corner, the eight-story building came into view. I made our way around to the back parking area and took a ticket from the automated boom barrier before it lifted. I parked and circled the car to open the passenger door for Lys, and she placed her hand into mine. It was a little out-of-body for a moment that the whole act felt so natural. I never hesitated or stopped to think about what I should do; I just did it.

After she shouldered her purse, I clasped onto her hand again, weaving our fingers together. I came to the conclusion a long time ago that holding hands with someone was intimate and reminded them that you were holding space for them. It didn't always have to be a romantic gesture, though, for me, it usually was.

My hope was that if the stalker was watching, they saw it and thought the same.

We made our way on the sidewalk leading to the mirrored glass front doors. As we drew closer, I watched a homeless man struggle to open a crushed bottle of water. I stopped and, by instinct, put myself between the man and Lys.

"Let me help you," I offered, lifting the bottle from his knotted and weathered hands. His white hair, while short, seemed to have been cut with very dull scissors, and his matching mustache and beard were yellowed from smoking and age.

He managed a sheepish, toothless grin, "Thank you, sir...it's darn hot out here. Gonna be a hot one."

Twisting the cap off, I pulled on the bottle, attempting to get as many wrinkles out of it as possible. I handed the thin plastic container and the cap back to him as he continued to mumble to himself about the heat. "Here you go."

"Thank you, sir...whew. You saved me from this heat," he smiled wider.

I reached into the back pocket of my jeans, pulling out my wallet. I didn't have much in the way of cash, a fifty and two twenties, but it would have to be enough.

"Hey, take this and find someplace shady to get out of the sun...maybe get some food?" I handed him the money.

His cloudy eyes teared, "God bless you! Oh...now, I can't take all this. You've got a beauty right there, you need this money—"

"Not to worry, friend. The lady is well cared for," I gently pushed his hand back as he tried to return the bills. "That's for you. You take care, okay?"

I finally turned my back on the old man and reached behind me to take Lys' hand. Her woody eyes shimmered as we turned the corner, approaching the entrance. For a split second, I had the thought that what I saw were... *tears* in her eyes, but as soon as we entered the building, they seemed to disappear as if they never existed.

We didn't have long to wait after the receptionist sent a message upstairs that we arrived. Taking the elevator to the third floor, Nicolas "Nighttime Nic" Diaz met us in the hallway.

"Ioan!" he yelled in his usual jovial way. "I was coming down to get you."

He held out his hand and I shook it, "How are you doing, man?"

Nic chortled loudly, "Man, I'm always up to some shit. You?"

"Not too bad," I smiled. "Nic, let me introduce you to Lyssie Blackwell...Lys, this is Nic Diaz...with," I paused. "What channel are we doing this for?"

Nic's laugh never waivered, "We're recording for Fuel...but, probably get replay across all the market and online. Nice to meet you, Lyssie." He turned back to me, "I heard some rumors—"

"Yeah, yeah, I'm not here for that."

"Ha! We'll see," Nic held open the studio door for us. As he busied himself finishing with the setup and finding another pair of headphones for Lys, I pulled her aside.

"Hey...I don't know what he's got up his sleeve right now. I'll do my best to keep you out of this...we're only supposed to talk about the album—" I tried my damnedest to smooth this over with her, but she cut me off.

"Don't worry about it. It'll be fine...I've already got a plan."

I didn't feel reassured, but it didn't matter; it was showtime.

Chapter Eight

Alyssa

"Hey all you freaks and geeks out there, it's your boy, Nighttime Nic bringing you the best this hard rock world has to offer. And we've got the man, the myth, the legend Ioan Johns from Obliterate in the house today!!" Nic whooped excitedly into his microphone. The three of us sat at a table in the padded room, large microphones positioned where everyone would get a chance to be heard. A fourth person, a woman named Carol, manned the computer. "Ioan! Thanks for coming by, man."

Ioan put on his biggest smile yet, "Of course...thanks for having me."

"Sure, sure," Nic glanced at a clipboard to his right. "Man, let's jump into it...when are we getting this new music? You all have been teasing it for the past few months. Any updates?"

"We're in the studio now! We've been working on it," Ioan paused to think.

I couldn't tell if he really couldn't remember or if it was showmanship.

"...for the better part of this past year between tour dates. We're off the road for the next couple of months, so it's go time."

"That's badass! Are you looking at a date later this year, then?" Nic pressed.

Ioan shrugged, "We'll see. The guys and I are particular about sound and form...we want to give the fans something that's special every single time. If it doesn't speak to us, it won't speak to them."

"Speaking of that," Nic continued, "What's your writing process like? Is it lyrics first or music first?"

"Depends on the inspiration. A lot of what we do stems from personal experiences...we're human and have human emotions and faults. That's what we mean about it speaking to us...not just the album but every minute detail," he shifted in his seat. I watched Ioan closely as he talked about his process and his music, and I started to see the difference between Ioan the person and Ioan Johns, Obliterate front man.

The contrasts were small. The front man was gregarious and arrogant in a knowledgeable way, and while the person was like that to a degree, he also showed a softer and more grounded side. I realized our bluff wouldn't be a hard task for him at all because he always had a different face to the world.

"Man, that's sick!" Nic chortled loudly. "And Ioan, you've brought with you your own model and artist, the beautiful, Lyssie Blackwell, today."

Lost in thought, I noticed I missed most of the conversation. I watched his eyes widen with a look that screamed he wanted out of this part, but I smiled reassuringly.

"Yeah," he took a sip from a glass of water nearby. "I have."

"Lyssie, welcome, welcome! We've been seeing a lot about you two," Nic leaned in close. "I've heard the rumors about how you met...are those true?"

I glanced in Ioan's direction, "Yeah...I mean...most of it."

"You're badass," he laughed.

I rolled my eyes playfully, "Well, it's not as it seemed...I got tripped up as this guy manhandled me...it was a lucky turn of events."

"So, what happened? Were you there alone? And some asshole just starts putting his hands on you?" he asked angrily.

I lifted my shoulder in acquiescence. Whatever blanks this guy wanted to fill in, I was going to allow. "I was with some friends and we got separated...I ended up closer to the stage, and yeah, he just thought he would try something."

"And, you saw this from the stage?" Nic turned his question to Ioan.

"Uhh yeah. Yeah," he stammered, a little in shock before remembering what he was doing. "That shit doesn't fly at our shows. Respect at all times...we want everyone, especially our female fans, to feel safe."

His words reverberated on my skin; that statement came from deep inside the person *and* the front man.

"Ioan, so, I know you all stopped allowing cell phones at your shows a couple of years ago, right?" Nic asked.

Ioan nodded, "We did. If you're gonna spend money on a show, we want to give you that...and you can't be in the moment when you're watching it through the screen on your phone. Live shows are filled with camaraderie and joy. Live in those moments.

"Right on, man! Yeah, you might as well stay home and watch something on your t.v." Nic agreed. "But, did not having a recording of what happened stop the police from getting this guy?"

"Not with a hundred witnesses around you," I laughed.

"How did you two keep this under wraps for so long? That's kinda hard, isn't it?"

I saw Ioan's face relax again, "You know, not everything is for the world. With the tour, we had to do some long distance...but we made it through. We had a lot of conversation about her relocating, and it was time to pull the trigger."

"Pull the trigger indeed! Hey man, we all wish you the best of luck out there...congratulations! If you want to catch more Obliterate, watch for that album in the coming months. Nighttime Nic out!"

It took around thirty minutes for us to say our goodbyes and promise that if we announced our engagement, we'd do it on his show. We rode the elevator down and exited the building in silence, and I don't think Ioan exhaled until we pulled out of the parking lot.

He let out a long, deliberate breath, "Okay, that wasn't so bad. Nice story back there, by the way."

"Me?" I huffed out a laugh. "That relocation story was," Curling my fingers to my mouth, I let out a kiss in the air, "chef's kiss. Perfection."

I cut a side eye in his direction.

"You're pretty good at this," I admitted. One of his broad shoulders lifted, then fell again. I got the feeling he wasn't going to admit that what people saw from the outside was just a piece of his personality. "Where to now?"

"I just want to drive," he replied quietly.

Pulling out my phone, I started a text with Bett, "You good?"

He nodded, "I usually drive to clear my head."

I had zero objections. My job was to be glued to his side; if his side wanted to travel from here to Portland, then I would too.

"Sounds fine to me...I can catch up with the rest of the team," I hit send on my text, and Ioan drove. Having no idea where we were going or where we were exactly, I watched the bedroom communities and suburbs of Los Angeles glide by my window. But, after about an hour, I had to admit that I was growing tired of the sightseeing.

"So, other than driving, what else helps you clear your head?" I was also bored with the silence between us. My job was to identify the threat, and to do that, I had to know Ioan.

He shrugged, "Music...reading...normal distractions."

His voice was distant, as though I was pulling him out of his own head and it took a lot of energy to reply. I allowed him to brood for another fifteen minutes before I spoke again. "So, dinner tonight. What time is that again exactly?"

Seeing his eyes glance to the clock, I added, "You know, I can usually be ready for anything in less than ten minutes. But I'm guessing tactical gear isn't the dress code we're going with tonight."

Finally a laugh and, "We're twenty minutes from my house. Is that enough time to add some glitter to that gun?"

Chapter Nine

Ioan

A few hours and two more interviews later, I heard the quick staccato of heels on the stairs as Alyssa descended. When I turned around, she almost took my breath away. I knew I wasn't supposed to think things like that about her; this was a business arraignment, and she was a weapon. But I couldn't help myself.

She wore a simple black dress that ended just above her knee and heels that brought her a little closer to my height. Her sparkling earrings were accentuated by the soft way in which she pulled her hair into a loose knot, tendrils framing her face. There wasn't a person on the planet who would question if she was a real model. Getting a little hot under the collar, I went to the kitchen to grab a bottle of water while she filled her purse with her phone, a house key, and a small handgun.

"Well, how do I look, Mr. Johns?" she asked from the door's threshold as she used a small mirror to apply a cherry red lipstick.

Gorgeous. My God. She was gorgeous.

And dangerous. She could probably use two fingers and stop my heart. I didn't know how extensive Onyx Industries trained their employees or anything about her background, but I figured she wouldn't be here if she wasn't a little...viperous.

"Marco is going to lose his mind," I laughed. "He has a thing for brunettes."

"Does Ioan Johns like brunettes is the question." Her lipstick case closed with a hard snap.

I took a large gulp of my water, "Uhhh, yes, I do. I mean...yes, Ioan does. Which is to say I...do."

Damn it.

I watched a sly smile spread across her full lips. I think she did that on purpose.

Narrowing my eyes on her, I crossed my arms over my chest, "Are you ready to go or not?"

"Yep!" her reply was suspiciously cheerful. "I think I've got enough glitter."

As promised, she and I arrived at Giraldi's in my sixty-eight Hellcat. As I handed the keys to the valet and opened the door for my date to exit, I heard Ezra's loud, distinct whistle from the front of the restaurant.

"Man, you took her out. About time," he laughed, then looked at Lys, "expect to have a letter from the HOA on the gate tomorrow."

She looked at me, and I shrugged.

"I'm Ezra, by the way, and this is my wife, Val." He shook hands with Alyssa as if they hadn't met days prior.

"Very nice to meet you," she replied, and her voice sounded genuine, as though she had forgotten about our act.

I wrapped my arm around her waist, "Marco here yet?"

"I think I saw Cassie as we rolled up, so Billy might be inside," Val replied. "We haven't seen Marco...so, maybe?"

Giving my friends a weary look, I sighed, "Alright, let's hear Mikal's proposal."

"At least he won't be here," Ezra said wryly as we walked through the door. "There's not enough wine in this place for that."

The maître d' led us through the first dimly lit dining hall to a private room around the corner. When he opened the door, Ezra and I exchanged near eye rolls. In the center of the room stood Mikal Stavopolos, the CEO of Siren Records, laughing quite loudly with our bandmates, Billy and Tomas, and their girlfriends.

"Awesome," I whispered through clenched teeth.

Ezra eyed me, "Where's the waiter? I'm going to need something heavier than wine."

But, as soon as Mikal saw the four of us, he turned his over-the-top frivolity in our direction, "Hey! There they are! Come in..." He stopped and looked dead-eyed at Lys, "Ioan, who is this lovely lady you've brought with you?"

As Ezra and Val crossed between us and him, I heard Val whisper to Alyssa, "Be careful...that snake bites."

She nodded to Val but turned on her brightest and *most fake* smile to Mikal. She held out her hand, "Lyssie Blackwell. It's nice to meet you."

"Oh, Ioan...a woman with style," Mikal cooed greasily and kissed Lys's hand. "Mikal Stavopolos, Siren Records."

I rolled my eyes but laughed cordially, "Alright, she's my girl, Mikal."

"Indeed," he purred, then winked at her. "Come! Let's have some good food...and celebrate another partnership."

Guiding her near a corner, we stopped to speak with others in the room. I introduced her to our drummer, Tomas, and his girlfriend Nina, and our bassist, Billy, and his girlfriend Cassie. Marco was our next stop, and I realized he had already had a few bourbons in him by the time we arrived, so talking to him was in itself an exercise in acting and restraint.

After mingling for a bit, dinner was served, and the band, our dates, the label's management team, and Marco sat around the long table. It was mostly small talk, and after dessert and coffee, Mikal caught my eye and nodded for me to follow him as everyone rose to leave.

The room was buzzing with light conversation as Mikal got close to speak, "Ioan, my boy...what are you doing?"

Ezra and Billy sauntered up as I replied, "What are you talking about?"

"You boys, all of you," he made an effort to point at each of us. "You need to be looking at your future. Your legacy, huh? Don't make stupid mistakes...you're not spring chickens anymore."

Billy smirked, "Are you calling us old, Mik?"

"No, but I am saying that you boys need to be thinking ahead. Do what's good for you...strategy. Billy, no more crowd surfing."

He was starting to sound like one of the Big Ten coaches.

"C'mon, boys! Don't do anything to jeopardize your futures...let's take this to the next level," he clapped me on the shoulder. "Look, it was great seeing all of you...I've got a plane to catch, something big in New York. I'll see you all soon!"

We shook hands, and he was gone. Mikal had no sooner left when Val and Alyssa approached, both women giggling.

"Are we ready?" I asked, and she nodded.

"It was so nice to meet you," she waved.

Lacing my fingers with hers, we wove through the nearly empty restaurant and met with the valet outside. Once inside the car, Alyssa kicked her heels into the floorboard, "That's better."

I felt her eyes on me for a long time, but I concentrated on the road and focused on nothing else but the soft music through the radio.

"That was a nice night," she said flatly. "Mikal seems like a great guy."

The comment snapped me back into reality and I burst into laughter, "Well, if you like overly paid used car salesmen types, then okay."

"Aren't record executives supposed to be brilliant? Have their finger on the pulse of the trends?" she offered in rebuttal. I wasn't sure if she was actually trying to defend Mikal or if she was looking for information.

I hoped it was the latter.

I nodded, "Yeah, I mean, he is, in his own way. He wouldn't have gotten where he is if he wasn't. But, a lot of his talent lies in the ability to kiss everyone's ass." I thought for a moment before I continued, "Mikal is self-made. He has zero musical talent himself, but what he does have is an ear for up and coming talent...he gets them on the way up and promotes the hell out of them."

"But you're still not a fan?" she asked.

I had to think about that answer as well. It wasn't that I *disliked* him. On the contrary, he was a very likeable guy when he wasn't micromanaging every detail of someone's life and career. Or hitting on someone's wife. Or throwing tantrums when he didn't get his way.

"Mikal's alright. As far as the promotions and marketing of talent, he's great. I just wouldn't trust him around my girlfriend." I paused, glancing in Lys' direction as I pulled into the driveway, "I mean, you know...if I had one of those. A real one."

Alyssa smirked as I turned to punch in the gate code, thankful that in the darkness she wouldn't see my embarrassment.

Chapter Ten

Ioan

The darkness of the room was no match for my brain.

How many cities do we need to put on the next tour? Should we do Europe or the US first? US... then Europe. No. Europe, then the US, so that the guys are home for Christmas.

I can't wait to find out who we can get to open for us. If I could have any band tour with us, who would it be? In fifteen years, we've been on the road with almost everyone.

I think I'll make smoothies for breakfast. Damn it. I'm out of bananas. I could probably order some now and have them here in time...

I rolled over, hoping that a different position would shift my mind off. It didn't. Reluctantly, I realized that the only thing left to do was get out of bed. If I were alone and not on house arrest, I'd go for a drive since that usually cleared my head. But something told me my girlfriend wouldn't appreciate a disappearing act in the middle of the night.

Throwing the blanket off, I padded quietly out of my room, down the hallway, and to the stairs. As part of my own security protocol, the blinds on all the windows were drawn at night, making every room especially dark. But, I finally found my way to the refrigerator and pulled out a sparkling water. Tossing the cap into the sink, I took a pull and leaned against the cabinet. It was then I heard the soft clang of the weight machine at the opposite end of the house. I looked at the stove's clock to confirm the time; it was two am.

"What is she doing?" I whispered to myself as I left my drink to make my way across the dining area and living room around a couple of corners, then through my office. It was a long way around, but I didn't want to frighten her.

I stood just outside the door watching her for a long moment. I didn't want it to be creepy. I just wanted to observe her. For me, Alyssa Salerno was a puzzle wrapped in an enigma, wrapped in a mystery, and I was fascinated with solving all of it. Squinting, I could see she had the Lat machine pulled down right at ninety pounds. It was impressive. Deciding that any more seconds I spent watching her could be defined as weird, I took the same path silently back to the kitchen. After all, she was a guest in my house and deserved her privacy.

The gym's entrance had two hallways leading to its door: through my office, then a long hallway winding around the rooms, to the living room, then the kitchen, or the shortcut running near the dining room. Just as I rounded the last corner from the hallway leading to the living room, I heard a loud click. Looking up, I saw a silhouette of a woman with a gun in her hand pointed at my chest. I immediately froze.

"Lys?" I growled hoarsely.

"Ioan?" her now familiar voice replied as she lowered the weapon.

I stalked toward her, "What the fuck is wrong with you?!"

"What's wrong with me? Why are you sneaking around the house in the middle of the night in the dark?!" she snapped.

"It's my house!" I bellowed incredulously. "What are you doing awake?"

She placed the gun on the side table near the sofa and drew a long breath. It was a sound that told me she was just as edgy as I was in the moment. The fleeting thought was strange, though. She's a tough guy with seemingly jagged edges wrapped in razor wire, why would she, of all people, be spooked by a bump in the night.

Alyssa dropped onto the sofa, "I should probably explain...I have a bit of insomnia. I couldn't sleep, I thought I might take advantage of your gym."

"No worries," I took the other corner of the couch, dismissing her apology with my hand. "You're free to use anything you need. For the future, the pool temp is regulated...perfect for a night swim."

Her silhouette nodded.

"So, what keeps you up?" I asked, hoping to finally have a real conversation with this stranger. I could just barely see her fingers picking at the edges of a throw pillow. In the darkness, she seemed vulnerable and softer, as though her tough shell was only a reaction to the daylight.

"Lots of things. Mostly my inability to shut my mind off," she confessed. "You?"

I nodded as if she could really see me, "Same. Right now, I've got all this tour stuff in my head. And smoothies."

Her laughter rang in the darkness. This was the very first time since our meeting in Vegas that I had heard her make a sound like that. It was clear and throaty and genuine. I continued, "Nietzsche would probably say we lack virtues and that has led to our sleeplessness."

I felt her curious stare in the darkness.

"One must have all the virtues to sleep well...shall I bear false witness? Shall I commit adultery? Shall I covet my neighbor's maid? All that would go ill with good sleep," I quoted the nineteenth-century German philosopher. "If you like to read, I have a small library in my office...help yourself."

She shifted in her seat but didn't respond. I felt the vibe in the room change almost immediately, and it was again all business, and her openness and willingness to engage melted into the night. Without saying a word, she picked up her gun, and Alyssa retreated into the darkness.

Chapter Eleven

Alyssa

It was late the next afternoon when the front gate buzzed twice before I could check the camera. Just on the other side stood a young kid, no older than eighteen, holding a long brown box with a large bow wrapped around its center. I hadn't seen Ioan since our run in this morning; I knew he was on the property, just not where at the moment. Reluctantly, I pushed the talk feature on the camera system's app.

"Can I help you?"

The kid raised his eyes and his hat in the direction of the speaker, "Uhhh...yeah. I have a delivery for a Lyssie Blackwell."

My spidey sense prickled, "Who?"

The kid cleared his throat, checking his phone. "Lyss-ie Black-well."

I didn't appreciate his tone, "Just a second."

Not trusting that this wasn't some sort of set-up, I jogged through the living room and left through the door leading to the pool. Ioan was laying across one of the lounge chairs, chest down with large earphones over his bald head. Circling around to the courtyard in front, I checked the wall as best as I could but saw no one. I tucked my Ruger in my jean shorts at the small of my back and slowed my pace to a stroll as I approached the iron gate.

"You.. Lyssie?" the kid stammered.

"That's me," I gave him my best Hollywood smile.

"No way! You're Ioan John's girl. Is he here?" the kid peeked through the gate.

I raised a brow, "That box mine?"

He nodded and I punched in the code to open the walk-through portion of the gate. After handing me the box, I signed the little line on his tablet. When he turned to leave, I stopped him, "Hey, here."

I handed him a twenty.

The kid smiled, "Thanks."

I reset the gate before following my path back to the house with my newly acquired gift. As I approached the door, I noticed a small card tucked inside the ribbon. Setting the box on the table near the grill, I pulled the card free and took it from the envelope.

My blood boiled.

"Goddamn it!" I snarled but as I turned to march across the yard, I ran directly into his wall-like chest. "Ioan!"

"Hey!" He laughed, "What'd you get?"

I set my jaw, "What is this?"

I flipped the card in my fingers to him and surprisingly he caught it.

"I don't know...but, if movies are to be believed, it looks like flowers?" he offered, fumbling the card in his hand.

"What the hell did you do?" I demanded. If he thought me leaving him in the living room early this morning was anything other than me being tired of his voice, he was mistaken.

He chortled, "I didn't do anything." Then opened the card, "Sorry? What does that mean?"

"Well, sorry is usually an apology for a slight. Like, oh, belting out the absolute worst of Nietzsche," I glared.

A wrinkle formed between his brow, "Hey, if I offended you last night, that says more about you than me. Regardless, I didn't send these. A hand delivery is more my style."

He winked at me.

A cocky little wink.

"You don't know anything about me," I spat back and was beginning to think I really wasn't the person for this job. But, before I could continue, my phone vibrated in my back pocket. Yanking it out, I hit the green button, "What!?"

"Uhhhmmm...I would ask what's gotten your panties in a twist if I didn't know already," Bett's honeyed voice snickered deviously. "It's got to be hard...with mister smoky stare. Ooo. No, I'm gonna call him Big Handsome."

Bett was the worst and best of all of us. I rolled my eyes, "Get to it, Bett."

She sighed once more as I walked to my delivery and fumbled with the bow.

"Okay, so, I looked into his calendar like you asked me to, but the only thing I've found so far is that there is a corresponding trip to Chicago either the night prior or first day and a return trip to LA on the last day marked."

"Hmmm," I mused, pulling on the enormous red bow. "Keep looking. I want to know the details of all of it."

I dropped the bow and wiggled off the lid. Inside were a dozen long-stemmed red roses. I glowered at Ioan who put his hands in the air and shook his head. As I reached inside to pull the flowers from the box, something slid by my hand.

Something...alive.

"Son of a—!" I screamed.

"What!?" Bett's voice clamored in my ear as Ioan stepped closer to peer in the box.

"Bett, let me call you back," I disconnected the call and stared inside. "There's something moving in there."

Searching the stainless steel pantry under the pizza oven, Ioan pulled out an extra long set of tongs. Carefully, he clasped the bundle of roses, lifting it out of the box. Beneath them lay a small, yet, no less angry snake.

"What the hell is that!?" I demanded.

Ioan tossed the flowers to the side, looking closer, "That, is in fact, a rattlesnake." He turned to me, concerned, "It didn't bite you, did it?"

I shook my head, "There's something else...hand me those."

Shifting the tool to me, I pushed the tiny snake out of the way to pull out a second note. I handed it to him on the end of the tongs to open.

"Well, I don't think this was just your sunny personality at issue," his face turned ashen.

I was still staring at the tiny killer reptile in the box, "What now?" Looking up, I saw Ioan holding the second note open for me to read.

Ioan is mine

I reached for the paper, but Ioan crumpled it tightly in his hand before throwing it back inside the box and stomping inside. My eyes darted from the snake to him. Carefully and quickly, I replaced the lid so the poisonous petrifier couldn't escape, then followed him.

I found him in the kitchen sucking the bottom out of a bottle of sparkling water. His intense eyes were angry when he saw me. We stared at each other for a long moment and I expected him to lash out or throw out any offer of emotion, but he didn't. After a few deep breaths, he tossed his bottle in the recycling.

"I need to go into the studio tomorrow...we're going to get most of the In Memoriam vocals laid," he said calmly.

"Okay," I nodded, "Let's get a plan together—"

"I don't need a plan, Lys. I need to work," his tone lowered by an octave.

"I know. I'm not here to stop you from doing that. But for me to make sure some crazy bitch doesn't Misery you...or worse, I have to do my job. You can't just run off on a whim right now," I explained firmly.

His fist came down on the island with a bone rattling thud and he immediately opened his palm in apology, "I won't be controlled by a ghost."

Ioan retreated to the downstairs music room where he stayed for most of the day. We didn't speak again until around eleven when we ran into each other in the hallway as I returned to my bedroom for the night with a cup of chamomile tea. But, even then it was cordial goodnights. I saw the annoyance in his eyes and I felt bad for him.

From what I'd witnessed and after spending this first week in his home, Ioan Johns was a nice guy. Was he arrogant? A little, but not as much as I thought when we first met. After all, he was undeniably talented, and he certainly didn't deserve any of what was happening to him.

Neither Bett nor Fox could come up with anyone who would want to do him harm. No ex-bandmates nor any of the very few ex-girl-friends. From all reports, he was always just as I was seeing him, and I couldn't imagine how anyone could want a man like Ioan hurt.

Still, the thought lingered that I was missing something because, for someone everyone liked, he certainly had an enemy.

One that either wanted him...or wanted him dead.

Chapter Twelve

Alyssa

Early the next morning, I woke with a splitting headache and a call from Fox on my nightstand. I really wanted to ignore him but, in my early morning sleeplessness, I remembered I was indeed on a job. Reluctantly, I scooped the phone up and hit the button.

"Fox, this better be good," I groaned, my fingers pressing into my eyeball.

He laughed wildly, and it pissed me off.

"Fox! I'm not feeling the greatest, so if you don't—"

"Okay, okay," his guffaws subsided. "I've checked out all four of the exes. I've got nada. None of them had a messy break up...everything was amicable, with the exception of one."

I was wide awake, "Who?"

"Slow down, tiger. Tessie Berber and Ioan didn't have a messy break up, per se, but she did have a lot to say about his *High standards with his women* and *Never taking his shirt off during sex*. She said it was *Weird*. Which, if the guy doesn't want to take his shirt off, that is a little weird." He paused, "Have you seen him without his shirt, Lys?"

I could hear the smirk through the phone, but my head was pounding so I ignored it.

"Well, as usual, your investigation skills are disappointing," I replied.

Fox's gregarious laughter filled my ears, "Well, you're in rare form today. I almost feel sorry for your pretend boyfriend. Or maybe I should feel bad for you? I mean, if an heiress like Tessie Barber doesn't quite fit the bill, a hot-tempered half-Italian girl from Seattle sure as hell won't."

"Oh, ouch," I finally had to chuckle. "At least you called me hot."

It killed my head to laugh, but it also felt good in my soul as we did.

"Alright, so, what now?" I pushed the heel of my hand in my right eye socket. "Any leads on anyone else? A driver? A gardener? How is the fan mail coming?"

"No, nothing right now...working on the mail. But, so far, it all looks okay," Fox sighed. "Other than what we have from our mystery girl."

I huffed out my frustration, "Keep me posted. I'll text you today's events as soon as I know."

"Sounds good," he replied. "Oh, and Lys?"

"Yeah?"

"Maybe a roll in the hay would take care of that headache. Tell Johns to take his shirt off first."

Tossing the disconnected phone back on the bedside table, I cut his raucous laughter short. Whispering to myself, "Such an ass," I threw off the blanket and rolled out of bed. It took me a little bit longer than usual to get even a little bit pulled together, but at around seven-thirty, I was upright and searching the kitchen cabinets for an over the counter pain killer.

No luck.

Coffee would have to soothe the ice pick drilling into my eye as I took my cup and my phone to sit by the pool. Before I could attempt to find a cozy spot, I saw Ioan, bare feet, t-shirt, and loose shorts, stretching his arms into the air as if holding the sky.

I watched his fluid movements for a long moment. He progressed through warrior, side planks, chair, and even camel pose. But, the most impressive was his crow; I'd never seen anyone of his height and build execute one so flawlessly.

Stepping just inside the shade of the pizza oven wall, I eased down into the overstuffed, round chair and resumed rubbing my head. Laying against the soft headrest, I did my best to not focus on the stabbing pain. I had to get control of this headache, if for no other reason than to put on whatever mask was needed from me today.

"Headache?" his husky voice asked.

With my thumb still pressed into the socket of my left eye, I peeked through my barely open right. "Yeah...it happens sometimes."

"Just behind your eye?"

"Yeah," I moaned weakly. "It's fine...I just need to find some pain killers. How close is the nearest drug store?"

"What you need is sleep," he corrected. "Stand up."

I looked at him, through my good eye, suspiciously, "Why?"

Rolling his eyes, Ioan held out his hands, "Come on. I'm not going to hurt you."

I groaned in protest, but sat my cup on the table and took his hands to stand. He pulled me into the early morning Southern California sun and a barb of pain curled my face. I recoiled.

"No, look at me," he ordered gently. I tried but the brightness of the daylight forced my eyes to close. Ioan put one hand on either side of my neck, softly resting his fingertips on my spine at the base of my head. Pushing lightly, he massaged the area with his fingers as his hands continued to support my head.

Once my neck was loose, he held my jaw line with his thumbs, "Look to the sky."

I did and almost immediately, the orbit crushing pain was gone. Opening my eyes wide, I took a slow minute lowering my head back down.

"Better?" he asked, smiling.

"Yeah. How did you do that?" I eyed him.

His shoulder lifted then dropped, "I have the same problem. Your body gets all out of whack when the insomnia hits. Have you tried yoga?"

"No," I smiled remembering his perfect crow pose and we stared at each other for a long moment. For a split second, I lost myself in his deep mahogany eyes.

"So," he said awkwardly. "I've got to meet the guys in Hollywood...we're finishing *In Memoriam* today. I'm not sure how long we'll be there...I mean, if you wanna check the place out then cut loose for a while..."

He almost seemed as though he wanted me to stay the entire day. Was he really that afraid? He didn't seem that way at all and as a matter of fact, he was quite defiant when it came to a threat to his free will. No, it wasn't fear, but there was something just under the surface; like he had something to say, but held back.

"I'm good to make a day of it. Just let me know what's expected and we can go over some signals I came up with last night," I replied. I'd been running our last conversation over in my mind all night, and Ioan was right, he shouldn't be fearful or controlled by something he couldn't confront. I would lure this person out one way or another, but in the meantime, Ioan had to live his life.

By nine, we were back in his Hellcat heading east on the four-oh-five to Neptune's Noodle, a recording studio in West Hollywood. Having just given him my list of signals we would be using from this point on, I thought a quick quiz was in order.

"What's the signal when we need to talk?" I sipped my fresh cold brew with cream from Little Bean.

Ioan insisted on making the stop and *paying*. I didn't realize what was happening and didn't have time to argue because when he rolled up to the window to order, he knew exactly what I wanted. I was a little impressed; Fox screwed up my coffee all the time. But, then again, that could be weaponized incompetence. And my partner was an asshole.

"A double tap in the palm," he answered correctly.

"Then?"

He cleared his throat, "I initiate close contact."

"Perfect!" I grinned proudly, taking another sip just as my phone vibrated in my hand. "Hey Wheels!"

Jake sighed, "Could you present a small amount of professionalism? Especially when with a client?"

I wasn't about to let him put a damper on my good mood, "Apologies, Mr. Merrit. How may I assist you this morning?"

I smirked.

"Enough, Lys. How's the head? Fox said you got another of those headaches again. When you get back to Vegas, you're having that looked at—"

"I'm actually fine," I admitted. "Better if Fox wasn't such a narc."

Jake sighed, "Lys, you say that...but you need to remember who you're talking to. I know you're not sleeping yet...which means unless you're downing half a bottle of pain killers with that coffee, then you aren't fine. You have responsibilities here."

I put the phone to my right ear in hopes Ioan couldn't hear our conversation. "Seriously, Jake?" I snapped, "I'm good. The headache is gone...I uhhh...well, Ioan showed me a trick and it worked. No dagger in the eye."

Glancing in Ioan's direction, I thought I saw a grin pull at the corner of his mouth. I hated admitting that I got help from *anyone*, but credit where it was due and all that.

"Uh huh." Jake paused, "Listen, I actually called for another reason. We've got a viable threat on Ioan's life. Are you still on your way to Neptune?"

Sitting up a little straighter, I nodded, "Yeah, we are. What's going on?"

"Continue to the location, Fox and Chico are taking a team in on the home to do a full explosive sweep," he replied.

"Threat level?" I felt Ioan's eyes shift onto me.

"Substantial. Assure Mr. Johns that everything will be as it was when you return," he paused. "On second thought, maybe you should take Mr. Johns out on the town. Give the team some breathing room."

"Understood." I disconnected the call and the air in the car was thick with anticipation. Figuring out how to tell someone gently about something bad was not my forte. "Look, I was thinking that maybe we should show ourselves in public more. How do you feel about dinner? Tonight."

He eyed me with suspicion, "What was that call about?"

"Threat assessment." I shrugged. "But, we really do need to get out there and you know...be seen."

"Yeah...I get that. It's kinda the point of this entire exercise. Why tonight?" he pressed, and I ignored him which annoyed the hell out of him. "Jesus, level with me. I fixed your headache after all."

I debated how much I should say. People usually react in only two ways when presented with a verified death threat: panic or anger, and both make stupid decisions. Then again, Ioan Johns was turning out not to be my typical client. He was level-headed, smart, and responsive to suggestions.

There was something else that I noticed about the world-famous Ioan Johns; he was unpretentious and *nice*. Two things that were, in my experience, difficult to find in someone like him.

"Okay," Shifting in my seat a bit. "We've got a team going into your house right now. There's been a viable threat against you."

His eyes widened, but never left the road, "A *viable* threat? What the hell does that mean?"

"It means we take every threat seriously," I assured him. "The team is going over the house with a fine-tooth comb...the best thing we can do is stay out of the way until they're finished."

Ioan was quiet for the rest of the drive, and I was beginning to think I might take back what I thought about him being level-headed. If he were trying to plan something, I'd have to be the one to stop him from making a decision that might actually get him killed. He parked the car outside of the squat building with the blacked-out windows and shut off the car.

He took a deep breath, "What do you feel like for dinner tonight? Japanese or Thai?"

Chapter Thirteen

Ioan

Neptune's Noodle looked unassuming from the outside, but once through the door, it was a cacophony of colors and artwork. A lot of people came through the studio over the years and they all left their mark. Paintings of landscapes, abstract sculptures, and candid photographs of musicians covered every inch of the walls and ceiling. I'll admit, when we first started recording at the location fifteen years ago, I didn't realize how much it would feel like home.

I led Alyssa through the heavy fire door separating the waiting area from the studio. Through another door and we were in the control room. Bear, our recording engineer sat at the large mixing console while the rest of the band took up space on the sofa.

I looked around, "Where's Ezra and Del?"

"Hit the head," Billy jacked a thumb over his shoulder as he flipped through sheet music.

"Perfect," I whispered before turning to Lys, "So, we're going to be in the live room laying out some vocals and music and I think we'll probably have to do some re-records, but we'll see."

We heard Bear's larger than life laugh bellow, "Not unless you screw this up, Ioan."

I chuckled back, "You do your job, and I'll do mine."

"My job's a lot harder than yours, boy," Bear chuckled, poking fun. "Who's this beauty you've got with you, Ioan? A good luck charm? You're gonna need it."

Bear Roberts was a master sound mixer and engineer who worked on our previous six albums. He was old school in most every way and a perfectionist. And while he was a little grumpy from time to time, there was no one else in the business that was better than Bear. And with Delmonico producing? We'd have a money maker for sure.

"Bear, this is Lyssie Blackwell," I introduced the pair.

Taking her hand, he put a peck on the back of it, "The pleasure is all mine." He turned back to me, "I heard you were shacking up with some new girl...no one said she was a goddess. Way out of your league."

He winked at her and although I was pretty certain she would never confess to it later, I was certain I watched her cheeks flush with color.

"Jesus, first Mikal, then you?" I playfully chided the old man, "Everyone's trying to steal my girl."

Bear dismissed me with a wave, "That dickhead don't have the chops to steal her. She's over his pay grade...he likes them young and stupid. Me on the other hand..."

Alyssa giggled, "I like you, Bear."

Bear looked at me, nodding, "I told you, boy."

I rolled my eyes and turned back to Lys, "So, this might be kinda boring—"

She took my hand right before I felt two taps to the inside of my palm. I don't know what it was about that touch, but it felt electric. So much so, that I almost forgot what I was supposed to be doing. I realized she was staring at me before I took her around the waist and we moved to a corner. I bent down so she could whisper in my ear.

"This isn't boring...and don't forget, I'm working." Her words were hot on my ear, "Besides, I've never been in a recording studio before...this is interesting."

When we pulled away I smiled down at her, lifted her fingers to my mouth and kissed them. A high pitched whistle filled the room. I turned in time to see Ezra smirking. The guys made room for Alyssa on the sofa as we headed in to record. Before the door shut, I heard Bear ask Alyssa if she wanted to listen. Evidently her answer was yes, because when I looked through the window, she donned a headset.

We recorded and re-mixed until six o'clock. Alyssa and I said our goodbyes and left the Noodle to find something to eat. Alyssa put her seatbelt on slowly and acted like she had something to say. I waited to start the car, allowing her time to collect whatever thoughts were running laps inside that beautiful head of hers.

But she didn't say a word.

Pulling out of West Hollywood, I made our way back to Santa Monica, and Alyssa was quiet the entire time. I wondered if maybe her team found something at my house or if Bear had said something that offended her, or he actually hit on her and he didn't take the rejection well. I would be out of character for him, but that didn't mean it couldn't happen. Although, I thought more about it, I wasn't sure she could be offended; she seemed pretty tough.

Maybe she didn't like the song. Admittedly, most of our songs were personal to me or to one of the guys and we always delved into the darker side. It could be that it just wasn't her thing. Weirdly, that idea made me a little disappointed because I *wanted* her to like our music.

Parking in front of Buddha Garden, I walked around to the passenger side to open the door for her. I handed the keys to the valet before lacing my fingers into hers and I did my own tap inside her palm. She looked at me puzzled.

Pulling her close, I brushed her dark hair from her ear, "Why are you acting so weird?" I leaned away from her grinning.

Alyssa burst into laughter. "I'm just thinking, that's all," she replied through a clenched, fake smile.

It wasn't my favorite, but even her false smile was beautiful. I nodded and lead her through the giant gold door of the restaurant.

Chapter Fourteen

Alyssa

In Memoriam

I stared at the end of your life,
A canyon on the precipice of which I stand.
The nightmares that you cause,
Some for which I will never awaken.
You dared me to become like you,
A demon for which there is no forgiveness.
Screaming unseen in the night,
Save me a place...because I'll see you in hell!
No broken promises,
Only broken wings,
No matter how you took your last breath,
I'll see you in hell!
Angels in their silent weeping,
No voice for the powerless at hand.
Your control is broken.
Grasping for the last of a haggard life now.
You dared me to become like you,
A demon for which there is no forgiveness.
Screaming unseen in the night,

Save me a place because…I'll see you in hell!
No broken promises,
(I'll see you in hell)
Only broken wings,
(I'll see you in hell!)
No matter how you took your last breath,
I'll see you in hell!
You dared me to become like you,
A demon for which there is no forgiveness.
Screaming unseen in the night,
No broken promises,
Only broken wings,
No matter how you took your last breath,
Save me a place…because I'll see you in hell!
I'll see you in hell!
I'll see you in hell!

As the music faded in the headphones, I was left completely empty. Ioan's words and voice haunted me in a way that was hard to describe. This wasn't the first of his songs I heard, as a matter of fact, I'd been deep diving into Obiliterate's music for more than a week now, if only to understand them and him. There were messages in their lyrics; deep meanings that evoked overwhelming emotion at times.

Like now.

For the past several hours, I was able to hear snippets: a re-recording of a verse or a riff. Or background vocals that Ioan laid behind his own lead. Bear accommodated me with every step and walked me through the whys something needed to be redone, or letting me listen to changes he was able to make. Deep base, breakneck guitars, pounding and heart percussive drums wove intricately with the lyrics. And, in the end, I heard it as a whole masterpiece, a perfect piece of art.

I allowed Ioan to lead me out of the studio and to the car. I felt like I was trying to grasp anything from my gut and make it into an emotion, but I still came up empty-handed. That song hit somewhere in my soul and resonated like a call home.

Before long, we were parked outside an ornately decorated restaurant named Buddha Garden. My mind was finally starting to shift from ego, life, and mind stuff to the reason I was in the car and why I was at this restaurant in the first place. Ioan entwined his fingers with mine and tapped me twice in the palm. When he pulled me close, I smelled his soft cologne; it was clean and woodsy.

"Why are you acting so weird?" he asked, a smile spreading across his lips.

He was getting good at this.

I laughed wryly and held a tight smile, "I'm just thinking, that's all."

I relaxed a bit as he held the large gold door for me, and the maître d' found our reservation before guiding us to the table. After deciding we would split a couple of dishes, Pad Thai and Tom yum, we settled in to wait.

"What were you thinking about?" Ioan sipped his water.

The question caught me off guard, "I don't know. I've got a lot on my mind right now...for instance, I'm scanning every face in here to see if I recognize anyone."

"Uh-huh. Why would you do that?" he eyed me skeptically.

"Why would I try to recognize anyone? Because if I've seen them before, that means they've been in your neighborhood or somewhere else the pair of us have been," I scoffed. "You're being thick."

"And you're being evasive," he threw back.

Damn it.

"Look, can we just focus on this charade we're playing?"

I was bobbing and weaving.

He smiled, then reached for my hand, "Sure. Right now we're on a date and madly in love."

I swallowed hard. And all I could think was why the hell my stomach was doing gymnastics. But I smiled back. Our waiter broke the awkwardness as he delivered our meal, extra plates, and refills of water.

When Ioan said this was the best Thai in the state, he wasn't joking. Everything was the perfect amount of heat, and the portions were more than enough for the two of us, plus a doggy bag. The arrival of the meal helped us relax, too. After a week of trying to find a rhythm that worked for us, we just fell into it.

We talked about favorite sports teams, and I was thrilled to hear he was a hockey fan like me. As a Bruins fan, I was happy to hear he loved the Ducks, and *not* the Maple Leafs, because if it were, well, we couldn't be friends. We also both loved watching a good action flick, and if it was made in the late-eighties or early-nineties, that was a bonus.

Once back in the car, I proposed an idea, "I have a thought."

"Okay."

"First, you've got to trust me. Can you do that?" I asked carefully.

He nodded.

"So, we know that whoever this is has some sort of access to you. And while they haven't been caught on any of your cameras, we know they're somewhere close. I mean, the leaked photos prove that." I paused and waited for Ioan's agreement. "I say, let's give them a show. Maybe we can entice this person into messing up."

"Alright," Ioan punched in the code to his gate, then pulled onto the drive slowly. "I'm with you. What are you thinking?"

"We should have sex."

Ioan choked, coughed, and slammed on his brakes, simultaneously throwing me into the dash.

"Uhhmmm...what? I mean, I'm not usually like...you're definitely attractive. Is that part of your job?" he stammered.

That was adorable, honestly.

Rolling my eyes playfully, I smiled, "Jesus...not real sex. We set up in your bedroom, back light it, make it look real."

Ioan thought for a long moment, "Like a video set. Alright, you're on Salerno."

Chapter Fifteen

Alyssa

Thirty minutes later, we were standing in Ioan's bedroom suite in pitch darkness. I wasn't a fan, but also didn't want to risk the stalker seeing us set up the illusion, so we had to fumble our way through. I realized this was the first time I'd been inside his room. Fox and Chico did a preliminary walk-through of the property and were here today as well, but I had never stepped foot in his space.

A king-sized four-poster bed in dark wood with matching nightstands sat front and center. It was classic, yet not at all overdone. Additionally, a comfy-looking high-backed chair stood next to a small wooden table on the far wall with a lamp, and just across was a door leading to an ensuite bathroom. It felt intimate but not uncomfortably so.

"Okay, so this lamp in the corner should provide enough light behind us to create the shadow on the shade," I explained. "Are you ready?"

He swallowed nervously, but nodded.

"Hit the light," I ordered.

Ioan did as I asked, and the lamp's golden light filled the room. I motioned for Ioan to come to me just as my phone buzzed in the pocket of my yoga pants. I knew who it was, and I knew he could wait.

Instead, I guided Ioan directly in front of the window and wrapped an arm around his neck. I slid the phone out of my pocket with my other hand and redialed Fox before tossing it on the bed.

"Looking good from here, Lys," his voice called from the speaker. Onyx rented a vacancy across the street and a half a block down from Ioan's and he and Chico were set up on the top floor watching. "If anyone walks by, they're getting a full show."

I slid slowly to the ground, kneeling for a moment before rising again. Ioan's eyes never left mine.

"Perfect," I replied, tossing a staged pair of pants. Reaching down, I disconnected the call. "Now, I need you to bend with me as I lie on the bed."

"I feel like I'm on display," Ioan chuckled. "And this isn't how I'd have sex anyway...I'd take my time."

My pulse was on fire. But, I cocked a furtive brow, "We're fully clothed and this is a ruse. We know that she's watching...we just don't know from where. If she believes you're *hers,* she probably won't stand for us making a display to the entire neighborhood. Besides, maybe we're just going to knock one out...you know, old-fashioned quick and dirty."

"What fun is there in that?" he roared with laughter.

Lying on the bed with my legs in the air like a Pilates roll over move, I laughed, "Could you just start thrusting the bed, please?"

He did, and we continued our play for about ten minutes before either of us spoke.

"How long can you hold yourself like that?" he asked with genuine curiosity.

I shook my head, "I don't know...like thirty minutes, maybe more."

"Humph," his tone approving. Or maybe he was impressed. I had to wonder if he was taking our play a little too seriously, and he wanted to find out how long I could hold my legs in the air for real. Or that could've been *my* mind wandering. Luckily, my phone vibrated.

"Yeah," I said in to the speaker.

"Lys, you've got a bogie headed your way. Someone just punched in a code on the gate and pulled up to the front of the house. Chico is trying to intercept," Fox said. "I've got visual...it's a woman, blonde hair, average height and build."

"Alright, Ioan, big finish here," I winked before I let out the loudest, most delightful moan of ecstasy. A devilish smirk pulled at Ioan's lips, and he did the same.

"Jesus, Mary, and Joseph!" I heard Fox yell. "Really, Lys?"

I giggled as the doorbell rang, holding my hand out to Ioan. "Stay here," I whispered as I flipped off the bed and shoved my gun in my waistband at the small of my back.

Bounding down the stairs, I rushed to the door to push the speaker on the camera system, "Hello?"

"Uhmm, hello?" a clipped voice came. "Ioan?"

"No...this is Lyssie. Can I help you?" I watch the woman flip her hair to the side and look completely annoyed. In the background, I saw Chico approach her and ask her to step away from the door.

"No! I won't! Who the hell are you?" she smashed the doorbell again. "I'm here to see Ioan!"

I opened the door just as Chico held out his hand, asking her to step aside.

"Don't you dare touch me! Do you know who I am!?" she wailed.

"It's okay, Chic. I've got this," I nodded, and Chico took a few steps back. I turned to her, "No, he doesn't know you...and neither do I. If you'd like to act civilly, I'd be more than happy to help you."

"I really don't care if *you* know me...this isn't your house, sweetheart. I'm here to see Ioan," she stepped her foot inside the threshold. But, using my body as a shield, I blocked her, and she stumbled back to the landing outside.

"Actually, it is my house since I live here. You're trespassing. So unless you want me to have security call this in—"

"Well, aren't you a little cunt? I saw you in the window...if you think that he isn't going to throw you away in four months...you're stupid too. Ioan knows we're meant to be together," an oily smirk spread across her lips.

I heard footsteps descending the stairs, and I wanted to throttle him.

"Tess?" he said over my head.

"Hi, baby. Can you make this...whatever... go away so we can talk?" she cooed. "Someone called me the other day to talk about you...and it brought up all these...memories. I miss you."

Ioan stepped in front of me and I swear the woman looked me in the eyes and sneered. She tried to put her arms around him, but he gently deflected the advance.

"Lys, this is Tessie Berber. And no, Tess...we can't talk. We said our peace a year and a half ago. I always wish you the best, but we can't be together...I don't have those feelings for you," his deep voice was compassionate, but weighted with finality.

She batted her long lashes, "But, Ioan...baby...we were always good together, right?"

"Tess..." he cautioned.

Like a switch had been flipped, her face became tight, lips pursed, "So. You're just fucking any whore now? Any little groupie? That's really gross, Ioan. Really gross. And weird." She leaned to the side to look me in the eyes, "I hope your little piece of ass was worth it. Did he take his shirt off? I bet not...I don't think he can perform with it off. So weird. And it doesn't even look like he broke a sweat—"

"Tess!" he ordered, but it didn't deter her. She was like a rabid dog looking for blood.

"Oh, fuck off, Ioan!" she yelled, throwing a well-manicured finger in his face. "You never had it so good! And this is it, I won't come back...ever. So, don't even try when you get tired of this cunt—"

"That's enough!" he roared, and Tessie Berber finally shut her mouth. "You will not come here and insult any of my guests, and you especially won't insult the people who live here. I don't know what you thought was going to happen, but it's not." Ioan reached back, lacing his fingers with mine. "I'm in love with Lyssie...and if I'd known her back when I met you, I'd still pick her. Don't come back, Tessie. And if I get one text message from your little brat pack, so help me, Tess, I'll tell your dad about the hotel in Barbados. Chico, can you show her the way out?"

Tessie's eyes went wild with fury, but she thought better of making an argument. Whatever happened in Barbados sealed her lips for good. With a gentle sweep of his hand, Chico motioned for Tessie to follow as he walked her to the car. Ioan and I stood on the landing and watched her taillights fade into the night.

We closed the door, and Ioan handed me my phone. I immediately dialed Fox, but he watched the entire incident go down over Chico's bodycam, so there was no reason to debrief. I wasn't sure if Tessie Berber was our stalker; she did have a motive and enough money to make anything happen. Or maybe she was just an angry ex-girlfriend who had some second thoughts. Regardless, I would make sure the team kept her under watch.

Chapter Sixteen

Ioan

"So, what's the story with Barbados?" Alyssa asked with a satisfied smile on her lips.

My God, those lips.

I realized I was staring, "Uhh, yeah." I shrugged, walking toward the kitchen, "She threw a raging party one night, and it got out of hand. The room was destroyed, but it was the bed in the pool, mattress and all, that sank her. Mr. Berber was about to cut her off anyway, and taking away the purse? Tessie wouldn't survive."

Pouring a glass of juice from the refrigerator, I continued. "Anyway, she told her father she was robbed. After hiring a boat to take her out about a mile, she dumped some of her least expensive jewelry, then filed a false police report. She also paid off some staff who knew she was lying. But, Daddy believed her and felt sorry enough for her, so he purchased a condo for her in Turks. For safety."

Alyssa stared at me, and I read the disgust all over her face.

"You're joking, right?" she replied dubiously.

I shook my head, "Not at all."

"Let me ask you a question then," her head tilted. "Why would you date someone like that?"

That was a very good question. I hadn't really thought of any time spent with Tessie as dating. She mostly showed up to shows and clung to me like glue. "Look, did I think I had feelings for her? Yeah. But it didn't take long for me to figure out the real Tessie," I replied.

Alyssa lifted a shoulder, "I mean, she is pretty."

"If you mean, outwardly attractive? Sure, maybe. But, none of it is real...it's a mask," I countered.

"You don't think women have the right to make themselves feel better with cosmetic surgery?" she argued.

I shook my head with emphasis, "I didn't say that, and that's not what I mean. People like her look nice on the outside...but, there's something wrong with their heart...if they even have one. That's not attractive, and that's not someone I want in my life."

Shrugging her shoulder again agreeing with me this time.

"Are you hungry? Thai food is great, but I could use a sandwich." I opened the refrigerator and pulled out meat, cheese, mayonnaise, and every other ingredient I could find.

"Yeah, that sounds good. I just need to make a call," she replied before taking her tablet off the bar and heading for the stairs. "I'll be right back...everything but mustard for me!"

Thirty minutes later, Alyssa returned wearing a long shirt and what I suspected were very short shorts underneath. Handing her a plate, I poured the pair of us each a glass of iced tea before offering her the bag of pretzels. She took a handful on her plate, then carried it and her drink to the living room, taking a spot on the far end of the sectional. I did the same but parked on the opposite end.

"Everything okay? That was a pretty long call," I took a bite of my sandwich. "Your team doesn't think Tess is my stalker, do they? Because that's out of the question."

She stared at me a little blankly, "Oh, no...that was something else. And I'm not sure...she certainly has the means and opportunity. Why would it be out of the question?"

I sipped from my glass, "Well, mainly because Tessie wouldn't have it in her. This has been going on for months...she doesn't have that kind of attention span. She moves from one trend to another more than either of us changes our underwear."

"Well, that doesn't take her off the suspect list...but, maybe it pushes her down a few rungs," Alyssa chewed her bite of food. "Thanks for waiting...you didn't need to do that. You could have eaten."

I scoffed with derisive humor, "Please...I'm nothing if not a gentleman. I wasn't about to eat alone."

She laughed, and we enjoyed our meal in silence for a short moment.

"I noticed on the calendar, you have a meeting with Mikal tomorrow? Anything I should know about?" she asked, sipping the last of her tea.

"Not really...just another contract meeting. He wants to make sure the ink on our new deal is dry before this next tour. It shouldn't take long...you're more than welcome to come, of course," I didn't want to ask outright, but I really did want her to ride along, maybe he wouldn't make a scene if she were with me.

"We need to be seen out more, I think a trip to your label is perfect," she nodded thoughtfully.

I took her plate and glass, loading them in the dishwasher as we planned our day. "I don't know how much time you've spent here, but we can do all the tourist stuff, if you want?"

Her guffaw was large and loud, "Oh, absolutely not. I get enough of that in Vegas. Besides, we're meant to be seen out...not swarmed by fans."

She had a point.

"Okay...so, maybe we run out to the pier. You can't say no to a corndog and cotton candy, can you?" I laughed.

She smiled a smile that lit up the room, "No, I can't."

"Perfect! It's a date!" I stopped short, knowing the mistake I made. "I mean...you know...for me and Lyssie."

She gave me that smile again. The perfect one. The genuine one.

Glancing at the clock, I just realized it was a little past midnight. I was ready to wind the day down, but somehow, I knew this woman would be pacing the halls for a few more hours. Part of me wanted to know why the night caused such anxiety in someone that their body would forego its essential need for sleep. But then I remembered why I often didn't sleep and why people I loved also didn't.

"I'm going to hit the sack," I announced, patiently waiting for any response.

Her smile tightened, "Sounds good. Good night."

She retrieved her phone from her pocket and began scrolling. Turning my back, I walked to the bottom of the stairs and waited. I wasn't going to pry into her life, but I did want to know if she was okay. I found myself caring a lot more about her than I probably should.

Turning back around, I called out, "Hey...if you want, go down to the theater room. The sofa is super nice and there are blankets in the baskets. Remote is on the table just to the right of the door, right under the light switch."

"Okay, thanks," she shifted in her seat to look in my direction. "I appreciate that."

I nodded and climbed the stairs.

Chapter Seventeen

Alyssa

I watched him slowly pad up the stairs and listened for the soft click as his bedroom door shut before I felt the disappointment set into my skin. Pocketing my phone and making my way downstairs, I curled on the end of the plush sofa, sitting motionless and in wonder as to why I felt the way I did. How in the world could I feel let down that he went to bed? It was an absurd thought.

Closing my eyes, I went through my nightly routine of committing to memory every movement of the day. It was a technique I learned while in training at Onyx that helped me retain important details that may come to use down the road. It was easy enough to get through the morning and the route Ioan drove to the recording studio. But, then, like a bolt of lightening, I heard his song in my mind. It's power and its haunting words tore through me and my breath caught in my chest.

What the hell was wrong with me?

From there, I couldn't recount anything except his face looking down at me as we played sex in his bedroom earlier that night. The game's goal was to pull out and hopefully, infuriate his stalker, and maybe it did. I still couldn't completely dismiss Tessie out of hand. She had plenty of money to make anything happen, and, as it turned out, it appeared she had a bit of a jealous streak.

Again, Ioan's beautifully handsome face came to my mind's eye. Damn it.

I refocused on the day ahead. While my meeting with Mikal Stavopolos was brief the other night, tomorrow I would see him on his own turf. I wondered how Ioan kept his label in the dark about his situation for so long. Would Stavopolos use the stalker to his advantage just for album and ticket sales as Ioan and Ezra both suggested? I knew most of the entertainment world could be seedy, but I couldn't imagine anyone would use a dangerous nutjob for their own gain.

My eyes grew heavy and I was quite pleased I was finally settling in for the night. I wriggled myself further into the soft cushions, crossing my arms over my chest. Closing my eyes, I wanted to drift into sleep, but all I saw was Ioan's smokey stare.

Why was I like this?

It was a question I couldn't answer, so I leaned into the fantasy. I mean, what harm was there? There was no denying he was good looking and even his arrogant grin was beginning to grow on me. I imagined what it would be like to have his large hands wrapped tight around my waist as my body melted into his. It was as if I could feel the tight ropes of muscle in his arms flex as his lips came closer to mine and the heat from our skin mingled into a surging storm.

My thighs began to ache but instead of pulling myself out of the illusion, I sank deeper into it until I could no longer recognize reality from dreams.

Chapter Eighteen

Ioan

I fell face first on my bed. I wanted to stay up all night and talk to her. It drove me crazy to think that I had this most perfect woman under my roof and I still knew virtually nothing about her. Did she even like carnival games and corndogs? I should've done a bit of my own detective work and found that out before I asking her out on a date to the pier.

But, it wasn't a real date. Ioan Johns, lead singer for Obliterate and Lyssie Blackwell, had a date.

Groaning, I rolled over to my back and stared at the ceiling. A fake date was better than no date, right? And, we would both be getting what we wanted. She and her team would get the public exposure they needed and I would get some time to get to know Lyssie, or rather, Alyssa. The problem would be the amount of physical connection I should use and that really worried me. I didn't want to cross any lines and had no idea how far we should go just for the sake of publicity.

I respected her, as I would any woman, and there were hard and fast boundaries and would be damned if I made her uncomfortable. But, if we were in a *real* relationship, I would want to the world to know she was mine and there would be very little space between us, ever. I would want her skin on mine every moment of every day.

I groaned again, and realizing my inner argument just talked my dick into a semi-attentive position, I rolled face first into a pillow; and that's the moment I smelled it...

Her perfume.

It lingered softly where her head lay just a few hours prior as we played a sexy shadow puppet show for the world. It also didn't do anything to slow my daydreams of her. I saw her hazel eyes staring up into mine like they had earlier, their green flecks glittering with mischief. The longer I inhaled her into my lungs the more I wanted to pull her naked body into mine and hold her there. I imagined what it would feel like to take a direct hit of her scent off her skin as I buried my face in her caramel waves.

Jesus, Ioan, get a hold of yourself.

I was being ridiculous. We were lightyears from anything remotely resembling my fantasies; for fucks sake, we were just now being friendly towards each other. But, even my rational brain couldn't overcome my desire to feel every inch of her under my fingertips.

Willing myself away from the pillow and off the bed, I took the coldest shower of my life.

Chapter Nineteen

Alyssa

Mikal Stavopolos's office was a sprawling open-air room filled with plush sofas, rich leather ottomans, and the largest mahogany desk I'd ever seen. Located on the thirty-eighth floor of a towering residential high-rise, the penthouse office was certainly luxurious but also a little tacky. Large canvas paintings in bright, psychedelic colors covered two of the four walls, along with an eight-foot-tall book shelf lined with awards and achievements.

"Mr. Stavopolos will be with you in a moment," a very young and underdressed receptionist said as she shut the large door.

I arched my brow, "Oookay."

Ioan chuckled, "We shouldn't be here long. I'm really just picking up my contract and the bands."

"Ioan! My guy! How are we feeling today?" Mikal entered the room with all the charm and showmanship of a circus ringmaster.

He was a tall man, just shy of Ioan's height, and I would estimate was six foot, two inches. He was fashionably balding, which was to say he didn't have a combover, and he wore a very expensive Brooks Brothers suit. The only way I knew it was real and not a fake was the golden fleece tag I spied when he shrugged off the jacket.

"Hey Mikal...I don't know if you remember Lyssie from the dinner the other night?" Touching my lower back, he reintroduced me.

Mikal apparently didn't see me or was purposely ignoring me because he shifted his eyes to me after pulling out his massive leather desk chair, "Ah, yes...the new lady in your life. Ioan, I was hoping we could have a private conversation."

Ioan's eyes rose, "Mikal, anything we talk about, Lyssie will just hear about later. We're free to speak."

"I honestly hope that isn't true, Ioan. I mean, c'mon," he waved his hand in my direction. "How do you know she isn't your press leak? Huh? This is what I was trying to tell you the other night, Ioan. Better decisions. Strategic. If you want to have a legacy like Mick or Steven, you've got to start thinking strategically. No offense, young lady."

"Oh, well, when you say it like that, no offense taken," I snapped back, and I watched Ioan's cleanly shaven head turn red.

"What the hell, Mikal?" he snarled. "Apologize. Now."

He waved a hand dismissively, "Cut your bullshit, Ioan. You aren't serious about this girl...you know that. Just like...what's her name, Tessie. At least with her, you had sense enough to screw someone with money. She looks like a starving artist."

Ioan's large frame took two strides to Mikal's desk, "You don't know what I'm serious about. Apologize, or you can shred all of those contracts."

"What does Ezra say about this? Tomas? Billy? Are they willing to sacrifice their entire careers for one piece of ass?" Mikal seemed unfazed by Ioan's aggressive demeanor, and I wondered how much longer I should allow it to continue.

"You think another label wouldn't kill to get us at their table?" he growled.

Mikal nodded, "I think they would do exactly that. Ioan, it's like beating wolves off of you. You can't trust anyone. I'm trying to keep you in the green here."

Ioan's eyes narrowed, then he turned to me, "Lys, can you wait in the hallway for a minute. This won't take long."

Rising to my tiptoes, I kissed his cheek before I walked out the door, "Certainly."

Five minutes later, Ioan strode through the large door with heavy footsteps. When we made eye contact, he looked...relieved. I tried to ask him in the elevator what happened, but he just shook his head. It wasn't something he wanted to discuss.

When we were finally in the confines of the car, he pitched a folder full of papers in the back seat. Closing his eyes, he took a deep breath, letting it out slowly. After a few moments, he opened them and then turned over the ignition.

"Ready for the pier?" he asked, his voice pleasant and calm.

"Ioan, we don't have—"

His soft fist bumped my knee, "Yeah, we do. Mikal's an asshole, and I'm not going to let him get under my skin. So...how do you feel about carnival rides?"

"I think a corndog was promised," I smiled as Ioan burst into raucous laughter.

After a short argument about who should pay for the parking, an argument I won, Ioan donned a Chicago Cubs baseball hat and dark sunglasses. Oddly enough, it didn't clash with his jeans, combat boots, and black T-shirt. We purchased tickets from a sweet teenage girl who would have looked more at home in a commercial for popsicles at granddads farm than anywhere in the greater Los Angeles area.

Our only job today was to be noticed. We needed people to believe that Ioan was in a serious relationship and deeply in love with Lyssie Blackwell. We walked the boardwalk, stopping to watch others play games. The air was filled with fried food, sugar, and salt water; it was fantastic.

"Hey! I love this game, want to play?" Ioan asked as we eased near the Water Race, a game where the player shoots a stream of water at a target, making their token race to the finish line.

I grinned, "No, that's okay...you go ahead."

Taking my hand, he double-tapped my palm and I drew closer. He leaned into my temple to whisper, "What's wrong, Salerno? Afraid I'll kick your ass?"

I laughed wildly, and it wasn't a show. "You've got to be kidding me. Not a chance in this world, Johns."

Marching up to the starting line, I took my spot leaning onto the barrier and aimed my gun. Ioan paid the attendant, took the place directly to my left, and tucked his sunglasses in his shirt. When the alarm rang for the game to begin, my trigger was already pulled, and that was the only head start I needed. But, Ioan Johns was a cheater and pulled out everything in his arsenal to distract me, including pointing his gun at me, drenching my backside.

I didn't let it deter me, and when the closing bell rang, I came out victorious.

"I believe that's a prize for the little lady!" the barker called. "What will it be?"

I looked at the array of stuffed animals, but there was only one real choice: "I'll take the unicorn."

Snagging the toy with his hook, he handed it to me. His eyes went wide with recognition. "Hey! Are you Ioan Johns?"

Ioan smiled, "I am."

The barker reached out to shake his hand, "I'm a big fan!'

He obliged the man, then pulled his sunglasses back on, "Nice to meet you—"

"Brandon," the barker filled in the name for him.

"Nice to meet you, Brandon." He wrapped his arm around my waist, "Thanks for the game."

From there, we walked the pier for hours. Playing every game at least a half dozen times, we were set to walk away with a lion's share of stuffed animals. However, after our second win, we started handing them off to a kid who waited in line. Except the unicorn. He would get a good home.

After corndogs, fries, ice cream, churros, and of course, cotton candy, my stomach was near bursting. The sun was just starting to set over the ocean when Ioan tugged my hand toward the Pacific Wheel, a one-hundred-and-thirty-foot, solar-powered Ferris wheel.

"Really?" I eyed him.

He shrugged, "I mean, it's the only thing we haven't ridden."

I nodded my agreement, and we loaded into a gondola. And it turned out to be one of the most spectacular views. From the top, you could see miles of coastline. The sunset's gradient from orange to pink to the gentle purple of twilight was magic, and I thought of Daisy.

Ioan tapped me on the knee, "You okay?"

"I'm fine...it really is beautiful," I refused to let him see me choke back tears.

"Yeah, it is," he replied, but he wasn't looking at the coastline or the sunset.

He was looking at me.

Chapter Twenty

Alyssa

I had to shake off whatever that feeling was, and whatever I thought I saw, or didn't see, because it wasn't real. Ioan wasn't looking at me, and he didn't call me beautiful. But the thought was like an earworm and repeated over and over in my mind for the entire five-minute drive back to his house.

I counted each second.

Everything would be fine. When we arrived at his house, we would say our goodnights, and I would pace until I fell asleep in the theater room like I did last night.

Ioan pulled into the drive, and I nearly jumped out of the car. I wasn't going to wait for him to open the door for me. But I froze. My eyes were stealthily eyeing every movement of every shadow. I took a deep breath, but the air smelled the same. I couldn't exactly put my finger on it, but something was off. I didn't realize he had laced his fingers with mine until he spoke.

"Everything okay?" he asked.

No. Everything most definitely was not okay.

The hair on the back of my neck stood on end and I knew we were absolutely being watched. Making two quick taps on the inside of Ioan's palm with my finger, I waited for him to respond. Just like we practiced, he stopped, wrapped his arms around my waist, pulled me close, and leaned in. My lips grazed his ear and his woody cologne filled my nostrils. It smelled clean and weirdly comforting.

Stop it, Alyssa...you idiot.

"She's here...watching," I whispered. "When we get to the door, pretend to kiss me...make it look real."

I pushed him back and giggled loudly before we walked to the door of the house, hand in hand, in silence. I listened intently for any movement on the other side of the gate. Any rustle of bushes. Any noise at all. I knew she was there, stalking, watching, and waiting.

As we reached the landing and the front door, Ioan again pulled me to his chest, "Make it look real, right?"

I nodded.

Ioan wrapped my face in his large hands and an electric shock shot down my spine. My heart raced beneath my chest, and I hoped he couldn't feel my pulse on his fingers. As his lips fell over mine, my core trembled, and logical Alyssa was losing the battle. But it was when his tongue ran across my teeth that I realized Ioan Johns wasn't just making it look real.

His hands ran down my shoulders to my waist and pulled me closer. I leaned into his embrace, sliding my arms around his firm waist and pressing myself into his broad chest. His mouth commanded my affection, and I was more than happy to oblige. Our kiss continued until we were both desperate for air.

As we slowly moved apart, we stared at each other for a long moment, both, I think, in shock. Pursing my lips, I turned on my heel, storming inside the house. Anger boiled inside me. How could I be so stupid? I'm always a consummate professional, and to have reacted the way I did in that moment was a new low for me. There was no way I would allow myself to have feelings for a client.

The click of the door behind me told me I could be Alyssa again. Stomping to the kitchen, I shed my small Ruger from my back holster, dropping it on the counter. I heard the whir of the shades being lowered, and for the first time was glad that I would be cut off from the outside world. The hair on my neck prickled again, but this time it was Ioan staring.

Pulling a glass from the cabinet, I poured myself a large helping of cold water. I took a long pull and ignored him, but out of the corner of my eye, I saw him cross his arms over his broad chest.

"What?" I snapped.

His eyes narrowed, "I was going to ask you the same thing."

I set my glass on the counter with force, "What the hell was that out there?"

Ioan's head cocked to the side as if I came from outer space. I had no idea how he could've been confused with my question. But the fact that I could read it all over him was infuriating.

"You told me to make it look real," he replied calmly.

That angered me more.

"Yes, Ioan, *look* real...not actually...kiss me," the sentence fell off my lips weakly as I still felt them tingle from what just happened. Ioan's eyes were cutting into mine like lustful arrows; slowly piercing me to the back of my skull. Arms still crossed over his thick chest, he took a step toward me.

"I think you liked it. That's why you're pissed off," a crease furrowed between his eyebrows.

I immediately took another gulp out of my glass as he continued to move on me like a hunter. He turned his head this way and that to force another eye lock with me. I didn't want to. I knew if I looked into his deep brown eyes, I would be lost. I hated what this man did to my mind and my being.

But I loved it too.

Finally feeling in control of myself, I turned to him, "I'm pissed off because you went way off script! None of this is real! I'm here to catch your stalker, nothing else."

He slowly crossed the remaining few feet between us, and the whole time I could feel the wheels turning in his head. This man wasn't stupid. On the contrary, he was probably more well-read than anyone I had ever met, outside of Jake, and knew most people better than they knew themselves after spending five minutes in the same room. Ioan stood so close I could feel the heat from his body on mine, and the intoxicating scent of his light cologne filled my lungs with each breath I took.

"Then why did you kiss me back?" he whispered in my ear, his hot breath sending chills down my spine. My eyes rose to meet his, but before I could answer, I saw something strange trailing along the wall behind him.

The small red dot, no bigger than a cat laser toy, moved along the covered glass wall just behind Ioan. As the neurons in my brain registered the danger, I pulled the front of his shirt and screamed, "Get down!"

As we both hit the tile floor, I snatched my gun off the counter, immediately releasing the safety. Within milliseconds, and before I could utter any sound of protest, Ioan wrapped me in his body and covered my head. Three gunshots screeched through the house and the glass wall exploded all over us. The next few seconds of silence that followed was deafening as I moved from under him and just around the island to look. Getting on the balls of my feet, the broken glass crunched under my weight, and I pressed my back against the island, holding my gun out in front of me. I glanced back at Ioan.

"Stay here!" I commanded. "Call nine-one-one."

"Lys...!"

I ignored him and made my way to the missing wall, broken glass crunching under my feet with every step. Always keeping something between me and whomever might be just outside, I was finally able to dip my head around to what lay beyond. But everything was quiet. Hugging the wall of the outdoor kitchen, I slowly made my way around to the opposite end of the pool. I slipped behind the decorative bushes lining the seven foot iron fence separating Ioan's property from his neighbor. It was there, just on the other side of the fence that I found the ground was disturbed and two spent cigarette butts.

"Lys?" I heard Ioan call out in the darkness.

I sighed out my resignation, "Here."

Rising from the bushes, I stepped back onto the concrete patio and met him halfway. His stalker wasn't getting braver, or even more brazen, they were getting more stupid. I just hoped I had enough time to stop what was happening before someone got hurt.

Or worse.

Chapter Twenty-One

Ioan

"How the hell could this happen!?" Marco's clipped New York accent bellowed from his small face on Lys's tablet. He was in a split screen with Jake. While I had no intention of including Marco in any of the side project with Onyx, Alyssa thought the news coming directly from the *man in charge* would sit better.

We just didn't tell him which team the man in charge worked for.

Jake shook his head on screen, "Local LEO's say the neighbor just to the west of the property is out of town. The suspect jumped the fence and took position just on the other side of the wall. By the time our people attempted to intercept, they were gone."

"What good is a security team if you can't secure anything!" my manager complained louder.

"Marco," I groaned, "I'm fine. This was probably just some random asshole."

The doorbell rang.

Alyssa rose, mouthing, "Stay there."

A few minutes later Marco was still making a scene about increasing security and how much it was costing, when Alyssa returned with a contractor and four guys with an enormous piece of glass. I wanted off this call and my opportunity came.

"Uh, one second Marco," I turned to Alyssa who was talking softly to a man in a white hard hat, "Lys, you're getting another call...from Kate?"

Her eyes widened but she pulled together quickly, "Just hit ignore on the screen, I'll call her back."

"Boy, you need to get out of town for a while. Keep your head low," my manager barked.

"Mr. Gatti, I think that's a great idea. I think we can find some place for a few days," Alyssa cooed as I watched Marco melt into her spell.

But I also didn't appreciate that everyone seemed to be talking around me, "I've got an album to finish! I can't and won't just pack up and leave to hang out in some hotel."

"Ioan," Lys' voice was oddly soothing. "I understand. But, we need a reset. Someone just tried to shoot you in *our* home. It isn't secure here anyway. Is there someplace we can go to give the crews time to do that, but somewhere you can still work?"

Her eyes called to me, begging me to understand her words. They were also pulling me in other ways and I desperately wanted to answer.

"What about the cabin in Big Bear for a few days?" Marco suggested. "You can still get some work done...and let them clean up this mess."

Lys's eyes widened, "That's an option. Ioan?"

This wasn't going to end. I knew I had to either agree or I'd never hear the end of it from Marco; but I also got the feeling that Alyssa wouldn't take no for an answer either. The cabin was a good idea. There were a couple of bedrooms and a recording booth, albeit a very tiny one. I nodded my head.

"Great!" Alyssa chirped.

Once Marco was satisfied with the arrangements, he disconnected from the call.

Jake cleared his throat, "Alyssa we're sending Chico from the heli-pad. I'll let you know as soon as the cabin is cleared. Ioan, we're going to need that address."

It took several hours for Chico to check that the mountain house was free of prying eyes and thugs with guns and I suspected he was doubling down on his own safety measures as well. Alyssa left clear instructions for Fox to closely monitor the workmen finishing the installation of the large, *bullet proof* glass walls before she climbed into my car and we pulled away.

Most of the three-hour ride was made in silence, with the small exception of the satellite radio which played soft in the background. After the traffic of LA proper, the road opened up around Del Rosa with the peaks of the San Bernardino mountains coming into view in the distance. I thought that this may have been a good idea after all; it had been a long time since I'd smelled fresh mountain air.

Making the turn onto Sand Castle road, the car made the slow and winding climb to the top of the ridge. My headlights flashed over the entry of the red pine home a little after nine. After pulling our bags out of the trunk, I threw my backpack over my shoulders and heaved the cooler of food up the staircase to the front door.

"The keys are in my pocket," I said. "If you wouldn't mind."

Lys' eyes narrowed, "Seriously?"

"My jacket pocket," I offered flatly.

Her hand slipped into the opening to retrieve the single key. Once inside, I took a moment to unload the cooler contents into the refrigerator before sloughing off my pack. I watched Alyssa wander around taking the house in.

"Nice place," she said.

"Yeah, it is. Good to use for a getaway every once in a while. There's a pool in the back, if you're interested. It's small, but nice. I usually take the room upstairs, but, if you're welcome to it..." I let my voice trail off. I wasn't sure how to move forward after the last twenty-four hours. Not only were we just shot at, but I *kissed* her. Part of me felt guilty, because she wasn't expecting it, but she kissed me back. That was an irrefutable fact.

Why did she do that?

I wanted to ask. But, after exactly twenty seconds, I talked myself out of it. The cabin wasn't the place for that conversation and I knew it may not matter anyway.

Alyssa shook her head, "No preference. I don't want to take your room."

"Either way," I shrugged. "Not exactly my room...just where I crash."

She looked confused, "Wait. This isn't your place?"

"Oh, no," I chuckled, taking a bottle of water from the fridge. "It belongs to the record label."

She nodded.

"If you're good, I'm going to head up. Long drive...and if I'm here anyway, I'd like to see the sun rise," I slung my bag over one shoulder. "Goodnight."

I climbed the corkscrew staircase and shut the door behind me before I heard a reply.

"Goodnight."

Chapter Twenty-Two

Ioan

T he trip to Big Bear was turning out to be a nice change of pace. The morning after our arrival, Alyssa and I hiked one of the shorter trails before returning for the car and grabbing breakfast at a local diner. It was there I learned of her hatred of fried eggs. Scrambled or hard boiled were fine, but she wasn't a fan of a runny yolk.

After we returned, I locked myself away in the small recording studio to write for the rest of the day. I only emerged around one a.m. when I realized my breakfast from the morning before was well past spent. I found Alyssa curled in a blanket on the sofa, with sitcoms from the nineteen-eighties playing softly on the television. I left it and her alone, made myself a sandwich and headed up to my room.

I woke early that morning and found Alyssa on the back porch talking and smiling into her tablet. It was apparently a very funny conversation because I saw her eyes brighten and her gestures become more animated with every second. I wasn't going to interrupt, so after sliding into my shoes, I headed out the front door for a quick run.

I never considered letting her know where I was because we had been attached at the hip for so many days I was losing count. Also, from the smell of the kitchen, she had already eaten and I really wanted one of the locally made donuts from the small gas station at the bottom of the hill.

I'd bring her back something. I wasn't a complete ass.

Making it to the highway and Martley's in record time, I enjoyed my sweeter-than-honey bearclaw and a cup of coffee all while shooting the shit with old man Martley himself. The place was an institution and Martley's son, Jonah Martley Jr., took over for the old man a decade ago. But, every once in a while, he'd shuffle in with his cane, sit at a table and reminisce with the locals, which usually turned into an all day affair. It was much like taking an appointment with the President. And it was my lucky day, because I beat everyone by about thirty minutes. After snagging one more bearclaw for the road, I began my trek back up the hill to the cabin.

Out of breath and sweating, I approached the front door, pulling on the handle. It was locked which was really weird because I didn't remember locking it behind me. But, again, Alyssa could have gone out for a hike, I wasn't her keeper, but, apparently, she was mine.

Not having my key posed an issue. Making my way around the cabin, I stepped onto the porch, peering through the sliding glass doors. Alyssa lay sprawled on the sofa as though she had collapsed after a long drunken night out. I wasn't an expert in the sleeping positions of Alyssa Salerno, but I had a sinking feeling this wasn't one of them. I pounded on the glass, "Lys! Lys!"

She didn't move.

"Alyssa! Alyssa, can you hear me?" I screamed, and still no movement. I threw my shoulder against the door hard enough that the frame pushed in, "Alyssa!"

I watched in relief, then horror as she tried to raise her head, only for it to fall back on the cushions of the sofa and her eyes to roll. I had to get inside the house.

Using one of the patio chairs as a bat, I hammered at the glass until, on my third strike, it shattered into a million pieces on the floor.

I barely stepped through the threshold, and the waft of rotten eggs slammed into me.

Coughing, I covered my mouth and nose with my shirt before scooping Lys' limp frame in my arms, "Alyssa...you need to open your eyes. Alyssa! Listen to me!"

I laid her on a lounge chair near the pool before digging my phone from my pocket to call nine-one-one. Within minutes, I heard the screaming of sirens as they raced to the top of the hill.

***

"Put the mask back on," I ordered as Alyssa sat in the back of an ambulance at the bottom of the cabin's driveway.

She rolled her eyes, "I'm fine. And I need to call my team. Someone just tried to kill you, Johns."

I stared at her in astonishment and watched as she reluctantly put the oxygen back over her nose and mouth. Was she seriously *working* right now? There was no way this could have been anything but an accident. There were only a small few that knew we were here and none of them were my stalker.

"Kill me? I wasn't the one locked inside a house full of gas," I argued. "Lys, it was an accident. I'm betting the pilot on that oven needs to be replaced...you just happen to be the last person to use it." I paused, "And don't take that off. I can hear you just fine."

"What are you talking about?" her voice muffled. "I haven't used that stove since we arrived."

"Regardless, this isn't suspicious," I stared into eyes that weren't convinced. "This place doesn't get a whole lot of use...and I know there have been some wild parties up here. Things get worn out."

Her eyes narrowed on mine, "Where did you go this morning? I came in to take a shower and you were gone."

"For a run," I replied quickly and continued since I watched the argument building on her face. "Just down the hill to the market. I talked to the owners then came back. I brought you a donut...but I'm not sure where it ended up."

Her suspicious eyes finally softened, "Alright. Well, thanks for locking the door behind you."

I felt the blood drain from my face and she saw it too.

"What?"

"I actually didn't lock it...I wasn't going to be gone long and didn't want to go back upstairs to grab my keys," I explained. A lanky paramedic peered around the door and we both became quiet.

"I just wanted to let you know that the fire chief is on his way down to talk to you. And we can head out with Ms. Blackwell any time."

Alyssa jumped off the gurney, climbing out of the back of the large truck, "Ms. Blackwell is fine and would like to head back home. To LA. Sooner rather than later."

"I understand that, but it's okay to be checked out...you could have died, ma'am—"

"Could have. But I didn't. Ioan?" her eyes spoke volumes. Loudly. And the message was clear, *'Agree with me because I'm not going to the hospital.'*

I jumped out of the back door as well, "Whatever the lady says."

The medic nodded, grumbling something about poor decisions, but both Alyssa and I ignored it and made our way toward the drive to wait for the chief. He emerged a few minutes later with the last of his crew and motioned for us to come over.

"Ms. Blackwell, how are you feeling?" he asked.

Alyssa bobbed her head, "Little bit nauseated, small headache...otherwise fine."

"That's to be expected. Listen, have either of you been doing any kind of work on this place?" The man's eyes shifted between us and we both shook our heads. "Well, okay...then it's weird. It looks like the hose from the stove to the intake came off. I know a company owns this house...any chance someone had workmen here?"

"I'm not sure, but we'll find out when we get back. We're headed there now," I replied.

"Sounds good. I'll have one of the guys put a piece of plywood on the window. Just have someone call the station when that line is replaced. We'll come and take the tag out." The chief handed me his card and left.

"Convinced now?" Alyssa whispered.

I nodded, wondering how much longer I'd have to look over my shoulder.

Chapter Twenty-Three

Alyssa

We arrived back in the city early in the afternoon. I was pleased to see all the work was finished on the house and everything was back to normal. Or as close as it could be for Ioan. After making a deal with Jake that Ioan and I wouldn't make any plans for the night, I took a long, hot, well-deserved shower and turned in early.

I stared at the ceiling in the dimly lit room. Usually by now I'm used to a new place, but for some wholly irritating reason, sleep eluded me. Like a dark mistress keeping me just at arms length so I would do anything to be near her, she teased and tormented me. Maybe it's this house? The shades over the windows still did me no favors. And who could blame me anyway after the last few days.

Grabbing my tablet, I scrolled back through my history for the Obliterate song list. After finding out Ioan writes most of the lyrics, I was even more fascinated to finish reading through them all. While the bulk of the songs leaned toward darker themes, I read a lot of references to personal struggles and healing. It seemed as though this man of metal had demons he battled every day and wasn't afraid to talk about it.

An intriguing and foreign concept for me.

I found from their first album *Disordered,* which turned out to be a study of the human need for violent release, to the most recent, that over the years their songs became more political and more powerful in both lyrics and musical style. In their eighth studio release, *Become,* the music was bolder still with the addition of some orchestral elements that complemented their thunderous drumming; one of their signature sounds. And Ioan's lyrics on that album were deeper and bone cutting.

> *I close my eyes in the darkness,*
> *I swim to you in the pain.*
> *Your laughter flies into my void, but it's the demon I have become.*
> *Ioan Johns, "Become"*

Wiping a tear from my cheek, I finished reading every word of their last album before refusing to confine myself to the bed any longer. If I wasn't going to sleep, then I might as well make use of my office amenities and get his words out of my head. Maybe a swim or I could just curl up in the theatre again.

I padded softly down the hallway, sneaking past Ioan's closed bedroom door. Hopefully, I wouldn't disturb him. I knew how unsettling it could be to have mortality thrown in your face and I imagined being shot at in your own home would certainly do just that.

As I made my way down the staircase, the sounds of a piano playing softly floated from the lower level but I was sure Ioan was sleeping upstairs. I released the safety on my gun and delicately descended the second staircase to the basement floor. As I got closer, I heard the melodic and muffled sounds of singing coming from the music room. My bare footsteps were muted against the thick carpet of the hallway as I crept to the open door and took a peek inside.

Ioan sat on the bench with his back angled to me but I could tell he hadn't been to bed yet; not really. Although unbuttoned, he still wore the black silk shirt I saw him in earlier and the dark pants were from today as well; the only thing missing were his shoes. I stood in unmoving silence at the threshold, listening as he played the canorous tune and sang softly to himself. This was a different musical side of Ioan Johns. There was no guttural yelling and no throaty reverberation. This was classically proficient, but no less haunting. I could barely hear the words, but some of what I understood spoke of some sort of deep longing.

Ioan stopped playing and I held my breath. I didn't want him to think I was spying or intruding in what seemed to be a very personal moment.

"You can come in here, you know," he called over his shoulder. "No need to lurk at the door."

I stifled a small laugh because his awareness of his surroundings was nearly on par with my own. I stepped into the dimly lit room and the wood floor was cool under my feet. Pulling a large wheeled leather chair from a corner, I pushed it just near the baby grand.

He noticed the gun in my hand, "Safety off?"

I stared at him, flipped the switch on as he smirked.

"You're still not sleeping?" he poked random chords on the instrument.

I sighed, "I'm getting there...just takes me a while to get settled into a job."

"Hmmm," he mused. "You've been here two weeks...one would figure that was enough time to get used to your surroundings. But, I guess when you're not comfortable in the dark—"

"What the hell does that mean?" I snapped.

He hit another chord before his eyes rose in my direction, "Am I wrong? I mean, it's okay to be afraid, you know that, right?"

My lips twisted in frustration and I refused to answer.

"I'm afraid of a lot of things," he shrugged while continuing to pick out a soft melody on the keys. "Right now, I'm afraid some crazy person is going to murder me in my own home."

"That's a valid fear," I offered with a soul cleansing sigh. I knew everything that happened over the past few days would be on his mind and I honestly couldn't blame him for being afraid.

Ioan stopped playing, turning in his seat, "So is yours."

I rolled my eyes.

"Look," he swiveled back to the keys, "You can dismiss me all you want, but you know I'm right. You like to put on this tough shell, Alyssa Salerno, but you're not a robot. You're a human being...you've got trauma. A lot of people do."

He tapped out another quiet song and I sat speechless. Nothing like being called to task about your past by someone who, on one hand, had no idea what they're talking about, but admittedly, on the other hand, was one hundred percent accurate.

"If you're wondering how I know," he paused to contemplate his next words. "I see it...it's not hard to recognize yourself in someone else."

My heart split into a million pieces and I felt my protective shield, my jagged outer facade, the only one I allowed the world to see, crack. I never asked him about his past and I never offered any piece of myself, my *real* self, to him. But he saw it. The darkest holes inside me that I thought were covered with years of shame and denial were as obvious to him as the light of day.

I don't think I could deny whatever feelings were brewing for him. Even if there was a gun to my head and the threat of survival loomed over me. Feeling the heat of tears begin to well in my throat, I bit the inside of my cheek to make them stop. I waited a few moments before I spoke again. "Ioan, I'm going to get this person. I swear."

He nodded, still pecking out his song, "Have you ever played?"

"No," I smiled.

His lips spread into a hint of his cocky grin, "Come here...I'll teach you."

Huffing out a small laugh, I sat my gun in the chair and took a seat next to Ioan on the bench. He positioned my hands and fingers over chords and instructed me to lower the notes slowly. I did and we repeated the game over new notes. It only took a few tries before my fingers mastered the positions and I could switch from one to another easily.

"I think you might be a natural," he laughed. "There could be room for you on this next tour."

"Surrre," I chuckled. "I think I'll stick to security work."

A silence fell between us while he continued to play and I sat by his side watching his fingers in wonder. It was truly impressive the way his strong hands moved fluidly over the keys, gently enticing the softest sounds from them. The music that flowed so freely from him in that moment was so different from what the entire world heard. Obliterate's music, while impactful and moving in a lot of regard, was forceful and loud and in one's face. This was lyrical and tender.

"Can I ask a question?"

He never looked my way but kept playing, "Shoot."

I paused, "How did you get into that kind of music? I mean...you play piano beautifully."

A wistful smile pulled at his mouth, "My mother taught me to play. She was a music teacher and always had dreams of turning me into the next Debussy or Pollini. I, however, was a rebellious teenager." He shrugged. "It didn't give me the same cathartic release that my music does."

In a strange way, I could empathize with the sentiment. I tried a lot of things in my late teenage-early twenties to find the release I needed for all the anger I felt toward my past. I picked fights with everyone and anyone, just to let go of what had built up. After my third arrest and assault charge, I tried bungee jumping and skydiving. Nothing dismantled my anger. That was, until Jake found me and taught me how to shoot.

"My turn?" he stopped playing to face me.

I nodded, "Sure."

"Okay," he smiled again. "Tell me what you like to do in your spare time."

"Seriously?"

He let out a chuckle, "Yeah! You've been in my house all this time and the only thing I've seen you do is work. That can't be your whole life or personality."

I immediately wanted to tell him no and had to fight off every urge in my cells to keep from doing it. For me, that was a personal question that exposed my life to someone I barely knew. But, I did know him, or was getting to know him and I had to remind myself this is how friendships work. I could manage a few details, but there were important ones I wasn't ready to tell. I wanted to be Ioan's friend and every second that passed, I secretly wanted more.

"I like to ride motorcycles. I've got a really gorgeous Indian Chieftain I purchased last year sitting in my garage," I paused. "I can cro-chet...self taught. And I like to read before bed sometimes."

"Reading is good," the smile never leaving his lips. "I bet you're a self-help kind of girl."

I felt my face flush with color, "More of a smutty romance sort of girl."

Ioan erupted into wild laughter. It was hard not to engage with his amusement because I knew how much of a contrast it was to what I showed the world. He cleared his throat as our laughter died down to soft giggles, "I've got another fear I'd like to confess to."

I raised my brow in curiosity. Inhaling a deep breath, he held it for a moment; as if he were working up the courage for a heavy task before he managed a short sigh, "My fear is that you'll never answer my question from the other night."

My curiosity turned to bewilderment. The last several days were kind of a whirlwind of police, clean-up crews, Marco's blustering, and firemen. I thought hard about what he could have asked me and he saw me struggling to remember.

"Before all hell broke loose," he continued hesitantly. "Why did you kiss me back?"

Chapter Twenty-Four

Alyssa

My heart dropped, went past my stomach and directly into the floor below me. I felt my entire body flush and hoped like hell he wouldn't notice. His dark eyes bore into mine and found my confession inside them; bare and exposed.

The fire of impending emotion clogged my throat, "I think you know why."

"Stop hiding behind those walls, Alyssa," he whispered. "*Tell* me why."

The quake I felt by him saying my name shuddered in my thighs and I swallowed hard.

"Because I wanted to," I admitted softly.

Ioan straddled the bench to face me completely, "So, if I were to..."

He scooted closer to me and had nearly caged me with his legs.

"Do something like this," his face inched toward mine as he placed a soft kiss on my lips. "You wouldn't yell at me?"

Rubbing my lips together, I shook my head.

"What about this?" he breathed as his mouth engulfed mine.

I returned his affection as our lips tangled in an electrifying dance. His slow movement was deliberate and I felt that bolt of lightening down my spine when he ran his tongue behind my teeth again. Wrapping my hands around his neck, I caressed his head with my fingers and his heat singed my palms. Ioan let out a gentle moan.

When we fell apart, his eyes stared at me with a dare in them. He never looked away as he pulled me around to him, placing me on his lap. His entire body encompassed mine as he wrapped his muscular arms around me, pulling me further into him. My hands fondled his shaven head as we stared into each other's depths. We sat in that position for a long moment and felt each other's breathing and the way our skin tingled where it touched.

Ioan's hands crawled up my back and into my hair as he pulled my mouth down to meet his. I think the entire house could have exploded and I wouldn't have noticed. I leaned my head back to look at him, if only to confirm that what was happening was real, but Ioan refused to allow his lips to leave me and he drew a line of soft kisses behind my ear and down my neck.

My core melted and I gave him a small whimper of pleasure.

Ioan pulled back, huffing out a short snort. Reaching around my back, he slammed the cover for the piano's keys closed. He looked at me with an almost predatory determination and it set me on fire. Rising from the bench, with me around his waist, he sat me on the covered keys and stood between my legs.

"I want to touch you," he growled softly and deliberately in my ear. "Can I touch you, please?"

My heart raced, because that is all I wanted him to do but my mouth released a shaky, "Yes."

Ioan's hands moved up my bare calves, leaving trails of gooseflesh in the wake. He softly massaged my knees before gently pushing my thighs further apart. Slowly inching closer to the edge of my silk shorts, his eyes widened in surprise when he found my entrance soaked and uncovered. His eyes fixed on mine wildly.

"I don't wear underwear to bed," I swallowed hard.

Ioan licked his lips.

"And you never will," he whispered in my ear as a matter of fact before plunging two of his fingers into me. "Oh...my...God..."

Grabbing on to his neck, I let out a moan, but before I could really take him in, and feel the pleasure his fingers gave, Ioan had me off the piano and around his waist once more. His mouth crashed into mine over and over as he carried me out of the room and up both flights of stairs. When we arrived at his master suite, he flung the door wide, slamming it into the wall.

Neither of us cared.

Placing me on the large four-poster bed, Ioan never moved away from his place between my thighs. After shedding his shirt, he pulled at his belt and button on his dark trousers and I watched them fall away leaving black boxer briefs exposed. Sliding his hands under my matching pajama shirt, he pulled it over my head then stared at me.

It was as if he was admiring what he saw. For a moment, I felt unprotected and self conscience, but his eyes filled with appreciation as if he had waited a lifetime for the moment to see me laid bare. A realization came over me: his shirt was off.

Why was that significant, again?

My hormone soaked brain was having serious trouble putting the pieces together, especially after seeing all of him. He was broad and defined and the beautiful artwork that encompassed his arms, just reached into his chest. Leaning over me, he kissed me again and we fell back on the bed together but the moment our skin made contact, the frenzy began.

Ioan pulled off my shorts in one swift movement as I freed him of his boxers. The tip of his hardened length grazed my entrance and I felt the dam release. Moaning, I reached for him with every limb, pulling him on top of me. I wrapped my arms around his back and felt something terrible and sad.

A tragedy.

My fingers gently traced a pattern of deep wounds from shoulder to shoulder. I didn't have to see them because I knew what it was; I felt the thick webbing and puckers of burn scars and skin grafts. I immediately knew why he never removed his shirt. A small lamp in the corner gave the room just enough light for me to see the look of apprehension on his face.

He was afraid of my reaction.

Wrapping my arms around his neck, I pulled him to my lips, kissing him without reservation or restraint. Our mania reignited and before long, I was clawing for more.

A throaty laughter emanated from deep inside him.

"Going after something you want?" that cocky grin pulled at his cheeks.

I narrowed my eyes on him, "I'm not playing games."

"Oh, neither am I," his eyes turned lustfully dark. Pinning my arms over my head, I felt his breathy words in my ear, "You're going to come long before I do."

I shivered with delight beneath him.

Rising up, Ioan flipped me onto my stomach, pulling my hips into the air until he had me positioned with my bare ass damn near in his face. He spread my entrance open and ran his tongue along its edges until it was deep inside me. Then, finding my swollen bud, he gently massaged it as he continued to explore my center with sumptuous strokes.

Feeling my orgasm build, I plead with him, "Please don't stop."

But he did; just long enough to turn me over on my back again so he could suck gently on my clit until rivers released and my body vibrated. He had me just on the edge of climax when I felt his tip press against me. I wrapped my legs around his hips and drew all of him inside.

The moment I felt his entire length press against my walls, I came apart.

"Yesss," he purred. "Come on me, Alyssa."

Bucking, I wanted to scream out my utter delight as he drove into me. Stars clouded my eyes and I bit hard on my lip as my core tightened around him.

"Don't hold back, Alyssa," he growled darkly. "Let me hear you."

I did, and it wasn't long until he coerced another lengthy orgasm from me. We were all flushed skin and sweat before I felt his body flex and stiffen. He slowed down to drive deeper, clasping my forearms against the mattress. And with a rumble from his chest, he bellowed my name, spilling himself into me.

"Oh my God," I panted, my hand lay over him to feel the rise and fall of his chest. I rolled over to face him, only to find he was already staring at me. "What?"

He gave a short shake of his head and brushed a wisp of hair from my face, "I have a confession to make."

I arched an eyebrow.

"It's been a while," he smiled.

I burst into rolling laughter, "Whew. Well, glad to know I'm not the only one on the planet going through a dry spell."

We lay wrapped in each other, for hours, quiet and dozing, until the soft light of dawn tried pushing itself into our solace. The first birds of the day were just starting to make their good morning calls when my eyes, just barely open, scanned my surroundings and found Ioan watching me again.

"Good morning," he kissed the top of my head as it perched on his chest. "Get any sleep?"

"Uh-hmm," I purred. "You?"

"Yeah, I did."

Propping myself so I could look at him better, I opened my mouth to speak, but closed it again. I had something I wanted to say, but I didn't want it to sound weak or stupid. He eyed me, waiting. It seemed like he hadn't taken his eyes off me since he carried me in there.

"If you have something to say, just say it," he urged.

I paused again, "I just wanted to thank you...for, you know, leaving a light on." I pointed to the small lamp in the far corner of the room.

The catharsis I felt with even that small admission felt ill-fitting, but good at the same time. I wanted to thank him for saving my life as well, but the words were stuck. Ioan held my face in his free hand, and we locked eyes.

"You're safe here. I don't need to know anything else right now as long as you know that," he nodded his head sharply as if that was the definitive answer.

I don't know why, and I couldn't explain it, but I believed him. And for the first time in my life, I wanted to tell someone everything.

Chapter Twenty-Five

Alyssa

"**J**esus," I mumbled under my breath.

It had been a little more than a week after Ioan and I slept together and our lives inside the house were vastly different than outside, at least for me. I relaxed more when the shades went down at night and felt like I could be myself. It was easier to laugh and have conversations when the world was shut away and since we'd already seen each other naked, some barriers just naturally faded. And while he never outright asked for me to stay in his room, he always waited for me to climb the stairs at night, and stood by his door as an invitation. It felt sinful and a little decadent in a fun way.

I was comfortable with our dalliance, but admittedly, something shifted between us. After a late night of watching movies in bed, I fell into an uncharacteristically sound sleep. I'm not sure how long I had been out, but a sharp sound startled me awake.

The room was pitch dark.

My heart raced as fast as my mind was figuring out where I was as I tried to pull myself out of the space between dreams and reality. My fingers danced along the bed but only found empty sheets. Feeling my body starting to panic a bit, I forced myself to take deep breaths.

"Alyssa?"

I heard my name called in the blackness of the room.

"Alyssa, are you alright?" The bedside lamp flipped on and my eyes squinted to adjust to the sudden change. Ioan stood next to the bed, a towel wrapped around his damp body and a look of utter worry crinkling his face.

He ordered again, before sitting on the bed and touching my hand, "Alyssa?"

"I'm okay," I shook my head, my heart finally falling into a normal rhythm.

"You were gasping for air," Ioan replied softly.

I laughed derisively, "That was deep breathing."

There was no way I was going to get into a discussion about my fear of the dark right then.

"Alyssa—"

I laid back down, rolling away from him. "Seriously, I'm good…it's late, we probably should get some sleep."

Feeling Ioan's weight leaving the bed, I closed my eyes hoping that I could force myself back to sleep before he shut the lights off again. But, it's what happened next that had me questioning my definition of what we were doing and what was going on between us.

After finishing in the bathroom, I heard Ioan's steps move across the room to the small lamp in the corner and the soft click of the switch as he flipped it on. Another soft click and the brighter bedside lamp was off. The mattress sank behind me as he slid between the sheets. I felt the heat from his chest on my back right before he wrapped his large arms around me and pulled me into him tightly.

I laid there for a long moment, considering whether I should sleep in my own room or not. I couldn't imagine why he would want to sleep in the same room as someone who needed a light on; it was counterintuitive, and there was no way he would get any rest.

"I promised you, Alyssa," Ioan's voice was soft in my ear. "You're safe here."

Our lives in the day were different. Every day, we made sure we were seen shopping in Beverly Hills or having coffee at a local shop. Sometimes we would catch someone taking our picture from across the street, not at all discreetly, but also keeping a respectful distance. Other times, we were blocked from his car and asked ridiculous and often offensive questions before having a camera shoved in our face. It was a mixed bag, and I began to wonder why anyone would want to be a celebrity.

I hated having people watch my every move and to be cooped up in a house, even one as large as Ioan's, was isolating. Then there were the myriad of demands from managers, executives, and assistants. It was exhausting just keeping up with everyone being paid to help you...and I was one of them.

Or was I? Things between us were different now. Had I made the biggest mistake of my life? Probably. I mean, it's not like we had a rule book at Onyx, but if we did, fucking a client was for sure on the *do not do this* page. I was so confused by what was going on between us. If it was just a one time thing, how would I feel about that?

Disappointed. That's how I would feel because I was really beginning to like Ioan. He was funny and kind and sexy as hell. I even started to appreciate his mild arrogance; that short-ended smile had my knees quaking every single time. And my dirty little mind wanted to submit to whatever fun he had in store.

Jesus! Why was this so hard?

Making life even more frustrating, neither me nor my team were any closer to the identity of Ioan's stalker. That was, until I opened my tablet and saw pictures of us in his backyard, lounging by the pool.

"What?" he asked, seeing my deep frown.

I flipped the screen so he could see. "Well, someone is keeping tabs on us," I replied.

"Goddamn it," Ioan huffed. "Where did you find that?"

"Bett sent it to me with a note that it's a still frame from a YouTube video...one of those drama channels focused on music and entertainment," I replied. "I mean, we're getting the attention that we need...but..."

He waited for me to finish as I flipped through several other photos taken on that day.

"Yeah?"

"It's just weird. We've been showing off all over LA," I concentrated on the image in front of me.

Ioan nodded, "Right...so, what's weird?"

"These aren't pictures from us in public spaces. These are taken here...it's odd. Who knew we were hanging out at the pool that day? You took a lot of phone calls, I remember," I prodded.

He chuckled, picking up his phone, "That was over a week ago. Let's see...I spoke with Marco twice, Bear, Delmonico, Billy, Tomas. And numerous texts with Ezra. I could have told anyone what we were doing. But, I don't think any of them is my stalker."

I nodded, "You might be right. But that doesn't mean they aren't in contact with that person and don't know it."

"Do you seriously believe that this is a six degrees of Kevin Bacon thing?" he frowned.

A stiff silence fell over us. I still wasn't sure what to believe, except that every day the list of suspects was getting longer and I wasn't any closer to the culprit. This milk run case was turning into more of a web and I had to figure out what strand to pluck to bring it down.

I finally shook my head. "I don't know...but I'm going to find out."

Picking up my phone, I started to call Bett. I needed her to cross-reference every associate of everyone Ioan had contact with that day. We'd already ruled out his bandmates early in the investigation, but that didn't mean someone wasn't still connected. Bassist Billy Tucheman was a thirty-seven year old, San Diego native. He had one marriage early in the bands career, but divorced just three years after his Vegas nuptials. The short marriage produced no children and he lived with his girlfriend Cassie Spielman, a thirty-one year old violinist with the Los Angeles Philharmonic Orchestra.

The bands' drummer, Tomas Rico, was born in Miami, Florida, but relocated to the San Diego area with his mother and step-father when he was six. Roughly thirty years later, he was unmarried but he and his long-time, actress girlfriend, Nina Alverez, shared a set of ten-year-old twin daughters. And even though Ezra was our initial contact, he and his wife Valerie were vetted as well. The only person still on the list and someone I was willing to put money down on was Marco. But, before I could dial, the phone rang in my hand.

Daisy.

"Oh, I need to take this," I stammered as I jumped from the sofa. "I'll be right back."

Chapter Twenty-Six

loan

I enjoyed having Alyssa to wake up to every morning, but what I really loved was Alyssa at night. During the day, she was studious and focused. Every movement had a purpose and a goal. When we were in public, her eyes were always moving, committing faces and voices to memory. I became an expert at reading even the smallest expressions, noticing the tiniest differences between the two versions. In the daylight, she was mechanical and methodical, but at night, she was all warmth and affection.

That was, until I started asking questions.

We lowered the shades on the windows early one evening and ordered a large pizza with everything from NYC Pizza Company, a little independent joint with the best thin crust outside of the northeast. We sat in the living room, the pair of us cross legged with a chess set between us.

After she won our second game, we leaned against the sofa, stomachs full and laughing at her mad skills.

"Where did you learn to play?" I snickered.

She shrugged, "Jake taught me."

"You seem really close...the pair of you," I mused, not intending my comment, which was purely observational, to be taken as an act of jealousy.

Her eyes rolled, "We're not like that...and you could have just asked."

I stared at her for a moment, "I didn't mean...I just meant to say that you and he seem bonded...like a family."

"Oh. Yeah, we are."

I seemed to hit a nerve. I wouldn't lie, I wanted to know all of this woman's secrets. I would push a little more, but I wouldn't risk a shut out again.

"So, how did you get involved with Onyx? Seems like a tough gig," Rising from the floor, I gathered our plates.

Alyssa was quiet and when I looked up, she turned away from me, to rebox the game. She didn't make a sound, but I wondered if she was crying. However, when she spoke, I couldn't detect any tears although she did wipe her nose.

"It's alright. The pay is great and I get to do some really good work." Another swipe at her nose, "And, free gym access...so that's a perk!"

When she turned to face me, her lips and cheeks bore a bright, almost chipper smile but something like trouble shimmered in her eyes, "Hey! I bought ice cream when we were out...want some?"

I nodded, "Sure."

Admittedly, I'm notoriously hard-headed and my gut was barking at me to keep pushing. But how hard? I wanted to know this woman, but I didn't want to go at her too hard for her to decide I was too much. I switched gears and talked about hockey, favorite vacation destinations, and pet peeves. Night after night we settled into familiarity, and night after night I nudged her for more, but when I got too close, she blocked me.

A few nights later and after a rather incendiary phone call with her partner, Fox, that ended in a fiery tirade of f bombs and declarations of frustration, Alyssa curled up on the end of the sofa and rubbed her forehead.

I had been watching her from the kitchen as she paced the office with her Air Pods in her ears, her face contorting with fury as the minutes passed. It was only when I knew she was settled on the couch that I crossed into the living room and knelt in front of her.

"Hey," I wrapped my hand around her calf. "Is the headache back?"

She gave me a silent nod, but continued to press her fingers into her temples. The soft whir of the shade motors kicked on, and I decided it was past time for Alyssa to have my undivided attention. I knew she needed to vent, because whatever her previous conversation was about had her tied in knots.

I sat beside her, scooting my chest into her back as close as possible. I wrapped one arm around her shoulders and scooped my hand under her butt, lifting her into my lap. I circled my arms around her, pulling her into me. She nuzzled her head between my neck and shoulder and sat quietly for a long moment.

"What's wrong?" I asked, feeling her tension release just the tiniest amount. It made me feel a little more secure in our new relationship that I could have that effect on her. I wanted her to feel safe with me, like she didn't have to hide and pretend she was in control.

Her torso rose in a long sigh, "It's so damn frustrating." Her words vibrated off my collarbone and her breath was warm on my exposed skin.

"Tell me," I lowered my lips to the crown of her head and kissed her. She tried to sit up, but I pulled my arms tighter around her. I wanted her to process her anger while feeling a real physical manifestation of support because I was absolutely sure that wasn't something she had before, if ever. "No ma'am. I'm not letting go. Just talk to me."

She relaxed again and drew in another breath, "This case...your case. Every goddamn time I think we're on to something, we hit a wall. I'm not any closer to knowing who this person is than I was three weeks ago!"

I ran my fingers along her spine, making gentle circles as she spoke.

"And," she continued, "my suspect list is getting shorter by the minute. This might be easier if you weren't such a nice guy."

That made me laugh, "I'm not sure if that was a compliment or not."

I sensed a little smile pull at her mouth, "Depends on the perspective."

Her head tilted, and I looked down into her beautiful face. I let my hand leave her back to stroke her cheek, and for the first time, I saw something akin to real worry in her eyes and it hit me hard. She was truly concerned she wouldn't be able to catch this person. I smoothed my thumb over the creases of her eyes because I didn't want to see them anymore or ever again.

"Ioan," her eyes going hard as steel, "I'm not giving up. I will find who's behind this. And when I do...so help me—"

Her voice trailed off.

"I know you will," I whispered, my fingers still caressing her face. "I know."

We remained on the sofa, my arms wrapped around Alyssa for what felt like hours. No noise, no distractions, only the sweet sound of her breath and mine. When she shifted, falling away from her rightful place on my lap, I felt the emptiness immediately.

"I apologize. You probably have something you need to do," she ran her fingers through her dark hair and huffed a laugh. "I'm sitting here wasting your time."

I was both angry and a little saddened at the same time. Why would she say something like that? She had to know I was crazy about her, and every single moment spent with her always left me wanting more, right? That she deserved to be taken care of and listened to and comforted and protected? She knew that, right?

I realized in that moment, she probably didn't, and my anger grew.

"Alyssa," I grabbed her wrist before she could leave. "You've never had anyone to depend on, have you? Maybe, other than Jake?"

Fury flashed behind her green eyes, but as quickly as it appeared, they softened once more. I had definitely hit that nerve again, and I didn't need her to tell me how accurate my assumption was. I didn't know her story or even their story, but what I was quickly realizing was, for whatever the reason, she was defiantly defensive of their bond. Jake Merrit was a lucky man.

Her arm relaxed in my hand, "No. And I'm fine with that."

"No, you're not," I tugged on her hand gently, and she sat next to me. "It's okay to have someone else take care of *you* once in a while. You don't need your walls up all the time."

I was pushing my luck, and I knew it. I figured at any second she would change the subject or maybe flat out tell me to mind my business. But the words never came; she just stared at me unblinking like she waited for the other shoe to drop.

My need to prove my worth to her, to show her I could be another person she could depend on, had burrowed itself into my bones. It was something that gnawed at me since I carried her luggage to her bedroom. This woman may be my undoing, but I would make damn sure she knew what love felt like.

"What is your favorite meal?" Brushing a strand of hair away from her face, I tucked it gently behind her ear. From the look of confusion, she had no clue where I was going with all this and I rather enjoyed the idea of keeping her on her toes.

"What? Why?" she replied.

"Humor me," I grinned.

Alyssa thought for several minutes, and I saw when she finally settled on an answer, "Steak Pizzaiola on bucatini."

Chapter Twenty-Seven

Alyssa

My phone vibrated as I descended the stairs. Bett's name and her anime profile picture popped to life on my screen. "Yes, Bett...whatcha got?"

"Oh my...don't we sound chipper," she cooed. "Does it have anything to do with that gorgeous talent you're getting paid to shack up with?"

I heard the teasing smirk in her voice.

"Bett," I replied with a mock warning.

"Hey...as long as you give me all the details later, I say have your fun, sister," she giggled.

My cheeks flushed. If she only knew. But then again, maybe she did. Betty Lee Tompkins was a master of information systems, sifting data, researching, and digging into someone's past. She was also painfully shy, protective of her friends, and a voracious anime fan.

"Bett.." I warned again.

"Okay, okay...give a girl a chance to live vicariously through her friend," she laughed. "First, I dug around on Ms. Tessie Barber and came up with some little factoids you might find interesting. Two, and more to your point, I think I figured out why our dream boy was making frequent trips to Chicago. And before you ask, no, nothing on the slippery manager...yet."

Peering into the kitchen, I saw Ioan working away on dinner. I slipped out of the patio door to pace around the pool, "Let me have it, Bett."

She cleared her throat, and I heard the clacking of her nails on her keyboard. "Seems like Ms. Barber was not only in Des Moines, Seattle, and St. Louis on dates that correspond with Big Handsome's tour schedule, but she also attended the shows."

"Bett, remind me what items Ioan received from the stalker at those concerts," I urged.

"Hmmm," she hummed. "Des Moines and Seattle were messenger-delivered notes with stuffed animals, St. Louis was a box of bird feathers."

"Gross," I replied. "Anything tying her to paying for the service?"

"Not that I can find. Yet." Bett sounded disappointed.

"Pull all credit card statements...including ones with her father's name. And have Fox run through all CCTV footage. I want to know every move she made while she was in town. Now, tell me about these trips."

"Alright...did you know Mr. Johns is *from* Chicago? And up until last spring, his mother was still living in the city?" she explained. "Of course you didn't because you wouldn't have asked me to find out...okay, moving on."

"Wait a second," I stopped her. "I thought Obliterate is touted as originating in San Diego?"

"They are. But, it seems Ioan only moved to San Diego right before they all got together...or whatever they call it. Apparently, Ezra Stanley , the—"

"Lead guitarist. Yeah, we've all met him...nice guy," I cut her off. "Had dinner with him a couple of weeks ago."

"Lucky girl...he's cute too...does he like anime?" she sidetracked.

"Out of luck, Bett...remember? Married, three kids. What about Ezra?"

She sighed, "Anyway, Ezra moved to San Diego first and seems like he talked Ioan into the move as well. A few months later, Obliterate is booking local shows...but the entire time, Ioan is making it back to Chicago every month, sometimes more. And before you cut me off again, let me finish."

Pausing for what I can only imagine was a dramatic effect, Bett finally went on, "Turns out, Ioan's mother...Meredith Johns has been in a care facility for the past seventeen years. Well, she was until she passed away last March."

"Oh my God," my heart sank.

"I'm not finished," Bett chided me. "All of that is surface level. The reason his mother was in that facility was because of a traumatic brain injury from a domestic violence incident. Seventeen years prior, it seems the John's family had a lot of internal warfare...all perpetrated by the father, Henry Johns. He was bru-tal. Meredith had only been to the emergency room under her own name twice, although I did find some Jane Doe records from other facilities that match her general description. Anyway, it was once when she had a broken wrist, no doubt from husband of the year, and the second when on November fifteen, two thousand eight, a nine-one-one call was placed by a neighbor reporting flames coming from the second story windows of the family home."

"A seventeen-year-old Ioan is then seen carrying his bloody and unconscious mother out of the burning house before running back inside. Minutes later, firemen on the scene pull Ioan out of the house, kicking and screaming. It seems as though he was trying to rescue a younger brother, a kid named Rhys. Rhys died in the fire."

I covered my mouth in horror and thought of the scars on his back. The revelation sank over me slowly, like sand falling to the ocean floor.

Ioan risked his life to save his younger brother and in return, carried a permanent reminder of his failure.

Bett knew how my brain worked and was quiet for a moment, allowing me to process before continuing, "Just so you know the whole story...Henry beat Meredith that night with the intention of killing her, the boys, and himself. He set the fire."

I wanted to scream.

"What happened to the father?" I asked impatiently, but thankfully, my research Queen didn't scold me this time for interrupting.

"Died in the hospital a few days later as a result of his injuries," she replied quietly. "Lys, none of this has anything to do with what's going on now. A year later, Ioan is in California and from the looks of it, paying his mom's medical costs."

Closing my eyes to think, I drew a deep breath, "Damn it. Bett, I'm striking out here. No one has a real beef with him...and now, you tell me he's a fucking hero. I'm just not sure where to go. Close the Chicago file...I'll think of something." We said our goodbyes, but when I turned around to head back into the house, Ioan stood not two feet from me, a fork full of meat at the ready for me to sample and eyes flaring with anger.

"Ioan," I commented, but he turned his back, walking into the house.

The wonderfully perfumed house that he was cooking dinner in for me. The scent of garlic, tomatoes, and grilled steak wafted into my nose when I entered and enticed my mouth to water. He tossed the fork into the sink.

"Ioan, let me explain," I soothed as I caught up to him.

Whirling around, he railed on me, "You had no right, Alyssa!"

"I'm sorry, Ioan...but I had to know. I'm trying to catch whoever is trying to hurt you. Right now, I've got no leads." I wanted to leave my feelings out of it, but it was hard. I hated myself for digging into his life.

"You don't understand! If word gets out..." he paused. "I keep my personal life out of the reach of others for a reason! There is too much out there, and I need to keep something for myself. I don't let the world inside."

"Ioan, you knew from the beginning that we would turn over every stone to get this person...that's why we're so good at—"

He narrowed his eyes angrily, "If I thought my past had anything to do with this, I would have told you! I gave you and Onyx everything...every name of every ex-girlfriend. Every club we played in...every itinerary. But not this. This was mine."

"I needed to know, Ioan," I stated again firmly.

"Then you should have asked!" his bellow bounced off every surface. "Why are you like this? You sure have balls when you play cop, but when it's just direct interaction, you've got your little team to sneak around and find out information for you."

I'll admit, I was a little taken aback by his words, but I wouldn't be deterred. "I have a job to do and I will follow any and all leads as far as they will take me."

"A...job?" Ioan's eyes were wild. "That's it? I'm a job. Perfect...it's good to know where we stand."

"Ioan, don't. You know things between *us* are...different," I shot back.

Ioan turned his back and started shutting off the stove's burners, "You can say that again. I've nearly begged you to open up. To tell me about you...*Alyssa.* But you shoot me down every single damn time." He faced me again, "I'm not a mind reader."

"Fine," I folded my arms over my chest. "What do you want to know? You wanted to know how I got into this job, right? Okay...Jake found me working in a bar in Phoenix. I had a black eye and a broken rib from a fight the night before...which apparently, he witnessed. He said I had a job if I could get my temper under control. I was in Vegas three days later."

He raised his brow, and it infuriated me because he was asking questions without saying a word.

"More?" I snapped. "Okay...Jake paid for my first apartment when I arrived. I was thrilled because it had air conditioning...a luxury I never had as a kid or adult. He also paid for therapy, because according to him, *'No one is that young and that angry without a reason'*. Then he taught me to shoot and bought me my first gun," I glanced at my Ruger on the bar. "Is that enough? Or do you need more?"

"Oh, I want more," his head bobbed in admission as he wiped his hands on a towel. "Because I'm not letting this go."

Pursing my lips in defiance, I glowered at him, "You're not the only one that doesn't want the world to know everything."

Closing the gap between us, his intense eyes locked with mine. We stood in our impasse for several seconds before he cut the silence.

"I'm not the world, Alyssa. I'm yours." Ioan tossed the towel on the bar and left me alone.

Chapter Twenty-Eight

Ioan

I almost missed the soft tapping at my door. After taking the coldest and quickest shower of my life, I lay back on my bed trying to wrap my head around *The Catcher in the Rye* for the hundredth time. But my annoyance and frustration got in the way.

How can I be so smitten by this woman? This irritating, bossy, authoritarian, commanding... protective, smart, beautiful, sexy, kind, woman. There was no one else like her and no one else I wanted but her.

The soft tap, tap, tap came again. I looked at the clock: two am.

Tossing my book on the bedside table, I padded to the door, pulling it open a little more forcefully than I intended. Alyssa stood on the other side, the flashlight on her phone illuminating the hallway. She looked distressed and almost fearful.

Reaching for her, I pulled her inside my room, "Lys? What's wrong?"

Her glassy eyes searched my face before blinking and coming back into focus. Was she sleep walking? Or maybe this was some sort of medical thing like a seizure.

She shook her head, "Nothing. I'm fine...I, uhhmm...lost my phone in the dark for a second. Left it in the kitchen. It's fine now." She offered me a weak smile, "I'm sorry to bother you."

"Alyssa," I whispered. "It's okay to be afraid of the dark."

She shook her head at me quickly, "I'm not—"

But she stopped herself, and I watched her will away the flood of tears I knew were right behind her eyes. We stood with each other in pregnant silence for a long time. I didn't know a lot about her, not for a lack of trying, but what I did know was that she was a survivor. We both were. We survived whatever traumas were laid at our feet, and we did it on our own; we were made from the same ethereal stuff.

I laced my fingers with hers and tapped twice on her palm. She looked up at me, and I felt her body relax. Walking to the bed, we sat, and Alyssa drew a deep breath.

"My parents were addicts," she sighed. "Meth, heroin, coke...whatever drug they could get their hands on. They functioned...sort of. Depending on where they were on the addiction versus sobriety roller coaster."

I stroked her hand, suddenly understanding her abstinence from alcohol.

"When I was little, I guess I picked up one of their needles or their stash...after that, they started locking me in a closet to keep me *safe* when it was time to get high," her voice shook. "They were messed up a lot."

I held her hand tighter. I never thought I could ease her pain, but I wanted her to know I was there.

"I remember spending days in a closet because they forgot me. I can remember thinking that I was going to die in there because they overdosed and no one would find them until the bodies started to rot," her mouth twisted as she fought tears. "When I got big enough to fight back, they just locked me out of the house. In the dark."

A single tear fell from her cheek, but before I could react, Alyssa swiped at her face in anger.

"When I was twelve, I found out that if I left my window open, just a crack, I could wait until I knew they were shooting up and sneak back in. But it didn't change anything, by that time we didn't have electricity...or running water. I was still in that closet and they didn't care. I ran away soon after and no one came looking for me." Rivers streaked down her face, and she didn't fight them off.

I rose from the bed, gently pulling her with me. She was limp and pliable and I knew she had no fight left to give. Turning the blankets down, I helped her lie beneath them. I shut off the bedside lamps and the bathroom light, but left the small corner lamp on. Crawling in behind her, I drew her into my chest and felt her shudder as her gates released and she sobbed.

I felt guilty that I had driven her to admit to me things she would have rather forgotten. I would live with it for the rest of my life if it meant she would feel some sort of freedom knowing she wouldn't be judged or left alone in the dark again.

I would never leave her alone because I loved her.

The world was still quiet when I felt her stir beside me several hours later. My eyes were heavy from the lack of sleep, and it took me several tries of forcing them open before it stuck. She was watching me, still curled into my chest with her hand over my heart.

"What time is it—" I started to whisper until I felt her warm fingers over my mouth. As if by instinct or by comfortability, I kissed them, and she closed her eyes, feeling every sensation as I did. When she finally opened them, she had a look that told me she had so much more to say. But I was done reading her mind; if she could finally let me in enough to see a past I already knew was there, then she was going to keep the door open.

She inched closer, putting her lips on mine. She kissed me, and admittedly, I returned it, but I wasn't going to let her skirt around what our issues last night were, so I pulled away.

"Alyssa," my eyes narrowed on her. "Tell me what you want. Say it out loud."

"I want you," she replied almost immediately, and a little bit of fear crept back into her eyes. I saw her uneasiness in the admission of emotion, but there was something worse in the background: the dread of potential rejection. I knew what that felt like.

"Why?" I was being a dick, and I felt bad about it. But, damn it, I needed her own ears to hear the words out loud. I already knew what she wanted to say, because I felt the same electricity, the same pull between us. But, Alyssa needed to hear her own voice declare what we both knew was true so she could believe it herself.

"Because I love you!"

My reaction was hair-trigger.

Rolling onto her, my body completely consumed hers. I tore the silken night shirt from her, throwing it across the room. Next came the matching shorts and I made brief work of those as well. Running my finger gently through her valley, I felt the sweet honey waiting for me to devour.

And I did.

I made her come apart at the seams as I wrapped my tongue around her clit, licking her swollen center. I got harder as she held my head between her legs and screamed my name. But it was when I drove my cock into her core, staking my claim, her eyes never leaving mine, that I knew I had what I wanted: Alyssa Salerno was mine forever.

Eventually, I felt the waves of intensity crash over me, and I drove deeper inside her. My need was primal. I *needed* her wrapped around every inch of me, and I *needed* to see her face when I finally spilled inside her. Rolling her on top, I sat us on the edge of the bed and she wrapped her legs around my waist. Brushing sweaty strands of hair from her face, I begged her not to look away.

She didn't, and that drove me to madness.

I pulled out and thrusted into her with force as my fingers dug into her voluptuous and perfect ass. Her moans of pleasure with each grind filled my mind with more delicious and lustful thoughts, and I wanted to expend every delightful drop of her tight walls as they squeezed around me.

Alyssa pressed her breasts into my skin, scraping her teeth along my neck. Fire shot through my skin, my cock swelled, and I drove into her harder. God those teeth. I needed them to sink into my skin.

"Bite me," I ordered her.

She did, and my cock strained inside her. Working my finger between us, I found her clit again and pressed my thumb gently into her. Alyssa bucked, throwing her head back, and her core contracted around my length buried deep inside her.

That was my undoing.

"Oh my God! Alyssa!" I growled into her neck as wave after wave of my orgasm rolled through me. I drove hard and ravaged every last drop out of us before we collapsed on the bed, panting and wrecked. I wasn't ready to be without her, so I pulled her back into me until she finally relaxed into sleep.

Chapter Twenty-Nine

Alyssa

His lips on my neck were the only way I ever wanted to wake up. Ioan started just behind my ear with a gentle peck, and I was wide awake, but I kept quiet. He continued moving his way down, placing soft kisses every few centimeters until he reached my collarbone. Then a small bite, and my thighs quaked. But I lay still, eyes closed, enjoying every sensation.

After covering my shoulder, he worked his way in the other direction until he reached that one spot just behind my ear, at the midway point, and his teeth grazed my skin again. I couldn't contain myself, and I broke out into giggles.

"Hmmmm," his husky voice vibrated on my skin. "You're finally awake."

"Since the first kiss," rolling over, I faced him.

He pulled back to see me clearly, "You're a tease."

"You love it," I smiled back.

"I do," he whispered solemnly. His intense eyes searched my face, "Are you okay? Last night—"

I stopped him cold, "I'm fine."

"Don't do that," he ordered. "I thought we cleared that air. Part of loving someone is being vulnerable...I meant every word last night, Alyssa. You can have all the walls you want in your work, and we can build them to shut out the world, but here...us...they don't exist."

He was right, and I knew it.

"Ioan, it's going to take me time...so, I need a favor," I repositioned myself on the pillow and read the skepticism on his face, but he nodded. "I need you to call me out. Like you just did. I've spent years pushing everyone away or keeping people at arm's length. It's almost like I don't know how to do anything else. But, I'll learn...I want to."

He nodded, "Okay."

"Okay," I bobbed my head, then lay in his arms until we heard birds chirping outside his window.

Ioan broke the silence, "I'm sorry about last night. I knew you were checking every aspect of my life to track this person down, but I didn't realize you'd go back so far. I should have told you...saved you the stress of an argument."

"You were right, I should have asked. But now that I know," reading his eyes, I looked for a sign that told me not to pry, but I didn't find one. On the contrary, he looked as if he expected me to comment or ask questions. "I'm sorry about your brother...and your mom."

Clearing his throat, I watched this larger-than-life man wipe at his eyes, and it shattered my heart.

"Rhys was a good kid. Would have made a helluva drummer...he was already a damn near prodigy at fourteen." Another cough, "Mom was...a saint. She took everything that bastard threw at her and never complained. But after that night, she wasn't the same...she couldn't speak or eat. She existed. Henry made out better than she did."

"How long?" I bit my lip. "Were *you* in the hospital?"

Ioan pulled me closer and I spooned into his side, "Right at a month. The donor grafts did their job, and my body healed quickly."

"What did you do after you were released? Because..."

A wry smile spread, and he looked in my direction, "Because I couldn't go home? Ezra's family took me in...they helped me find a place for mom and with Rhys' funeral. They're fantastic people...one of the things I'm grateful for is their understanding. I got lucky because Henry at least left me a sizable life insurance payout. It was enough to cover services and mom's care for a couple of years...until I could make some money."

"You took care of her, didn't you?" I clearly knew the answer, but I didn't know if Ioan understood how much of an exception to the rule he was.

"Yeah."

I was amazed at how much of a heart this man had inside. A man who stood on a stage singing about revolutions and demons and fighting back with a guttural roar at level one hundred intensity. The world saw a force of nature. I saw a gentle rain on a quiet day.

"And Ezra never told? He's never talked about it?" I asked.

Ioan's head shook on the pillow, "No...he understands how important it is to separate our private lives from our public ones."

"That's a good friend."

"Yeah...it's the same reason why he rarely talks about Val or the kids in interviews. Fame is hard on us...but it's harder on the family," he admitted.

I was feeling so guilty for not sharing with him the most intimate parts of myself, outside of my past. The best part. The part that made me not the ice queen that he met a couple of weeks ago, but warm and cozy like hot chocolate in autumn.

"I have something I need to tell you," my throat felt like the Vegas desert. "About my life outside Onyx."

Rolling to his side, Ioan propped himself up on his elbow and arched his brow. "Oh yeah? Sounds scandalous. Is it?" his cocky grin returned.

"No, actually, it's not," I was second-guessing my decision to share.

Ioan read the concern on my face, and his eyes mirrored mine. He touched my chin with his finger, "Alyssa, what is it? Tell me."

"I have a daughter," I whispered. "Daisy."

My heart was racing so fast I thought I might vomit. Daisy was the single most important person in my life. Everything I did was all for her. But I found myself caring for Ioan Johns more than I had for anyone outside her. I was serious about what I said to him last night. I did love him. If he couldn't accept her *and* me, then I would finish this case with a broken heart, but I'd still be her mom.

I watched his eyes fill with surprise and waited for him to take back everything he said. But he didn't.

"Really? That's awesome!" he laughed. "How old is she?"

"Three," I replied, a little apprehensive.

"That's a cool age. Ezra's middle boy just turned four," his smile never fading.

I stared at him for a long time, waiting for the other shoe to drop. It was as if he was excited about her or maybe relief? I was having a hard time justifying his nonchalant acceptance.

Ioan's eyes narrowed on me, "Why are you looking at me like that?"

"I mean," I paused. "You seem okay with it."

"Because I am." He chortled, "I'm not delusional, you've had other relationships. It's no big deal."

I shook my head, "It's not like that...I adopted Daisy."

"Wow," his eyes eased, and his smile softened. "That's...you're amazing. Can I ask about her? How? Why?"

"She was involved in one of our cases. Onyx was hired by someone connected to UNLV Medical School. They gave information about a potential situation at a foster home on a compound outside the city. Apparently, a couple of the older children brought a young girl into the emergency room with burns to her legs. The staff started asking questions, and within forty-eight hours, we were on the case, working with state case managers." Feeling tears well in my eyes, I paused to fight them off. "We pulled twenty-two kids from that place...the youngest was six months old. All of them had undergone some sort of abuse by the foster parents...not to mention the fact they were all living in filthy conditions."

Anger flared in Ioan's eyes, "And Daisy was there?"

"She was the catalyst. One of those old space heaters fell on her while she tried to reach her bottle. She was a year old," I snarled. "I sat with her for a week in the hospital while her burns healed. Jake helped me with the adoption paperwork...he knew a judge who would look beyond my past and see I could give her a good home."

"Is she alright? Now?"

I smiled, "She's perfect. I have a nanny, Kate, who stays with her, and Jake, Bett, Chico, Fox...all love her and have put in the time with me. I'm going to give her the life she deserves."

Lying his head on the pillow, his eyes glittered with a smile, "You're the rockstar, you know that, right?"

I didn't know how to respond, and while they were appreciated, compliments were hard. So I turned to the only thing I knew, a firm ultimatum.

"If this is all too much for you, that's fine," I said, a little cooler than I really intended. "But if you're serious, then she and I...package deal."

"What makes you think that I'm not serious?" his smokey eyes squinted.

I realized I touched a nerve, but before I could explain or even take a breath, Ioan continued.

"You think I'm just here having a good time with you?" He sat up again, opened his mouth, then stopped. "Black ripped jeans, AC/DC tank, silver hoops."

I blinked, "What?"

"That's what you were wearing a year ago at my show," he replied sharply.

My heart raced and I felt it in my bones. "I know you make the crowd sleeve their phones...but you've probably got video of the show, right?"

"There isn't a video of the unicorn charm you had tied to your boots that night!" he snapped, the whole room eerily still.

"How do you remember that? And how did you see that?" I asked, truly full of awe. It was a tiny silver charm that hung from my bootlace. Daisy had a matching one on a necklace. Our own little good luck charms.

"When I came to the medical tent that night," his voice soft. "You don't understand, Alyssa. You completely blew me off that night...no one does that. You couldn't have given two shits about who I was or what I could do for you or any of it. It's that night I remember most. It's that night that I realized I wanted a woman like you in my life. When you sat across from me at that conference table weeks ago? I couldn't believe it."

His eyes drove into me as he paused.

"I've been looking for you my whole life. I told you, I'm not playing games. So, yeah, Alyssa, I'm serious about all of it. Are you?"

Chapter Thirty

Ioan

I have never showered with a more beautiful woman than her. And if we hadn't had other appointments to keep, which included a birthday party, I would have had her for hours in that tile and glass sanctuary. Just watching the soap fall off her breasts and hips like a waterfall, while on my knees, I made her cry out my name to the universe again.

As Alyssa dressed in her bedroom, I grabbed a shirt and shorts before heading down to the kitchen for coffee. Even though it was well into the afternoon, I placed a breakfast order of waffles and bacon with the local cafe before stepping outside to grab my delivery of newspapers and entertainment rags.

I preferred a newspaper to the internet; there's just something tactilely satisfying about turning pages and the sound it makes when you flip it open.

Staring at the cover of Bender, a weekly magazine dedicated to music gossip, I almost couldn't believe what I was seeing. The picture was of Alyssa, taken with what I knew was a telephoto lens, as the edges were a little fuzzy and almost pixelated. The bold headline over her head read:

MEET THE OBLITERATE YOKO ONO

The boiling blood started in my toes before shooting into my skull. But before I could react, something caught my eye; her outfit. I recognized where I saw her wearing the waist hugging jeans and pink cropped shirt. And as quickly as I was to anger, fear seeped inside.

I was so preoccupied with the realization, I never heard Alyssa descend the stairs.

"Alyssa!" I yelled before turning and bumping into her

She chuckled, "Yeah, right here...no need to shout."

"Look at this!" I thrust the magazine into her hands. She read over the headline and a wrinkle formed between her brows.

"Hmmmm," she mused.

Jabbing my finger at the paper, I growled, "That was taken outside Mikal's office."

"I can see that," her lips tight as her round eyes looked up at me. "With again, a telephoto lens. From what Bett said, the photos could be taken from a mile away. My question is how it ended up in this magazine."

"Why is this person following us?" I replied. "How do they know where I am?"

She nodded, handing it back to me, "Another good question. Have you ever had a run in with a reporter or a paparazzi?"

"No, I can honestly say in fifteen years, I haven't. Do I find them annoying as hell? Yes. But, they have a job to do and so do we," I shook my head.

Alyssa thought for a moment longer, "I'll send it in regardless. Bett might be able to tell us a general direction that the photo was taken...maybe get some CCTV footage if she is able to triangulate."

She didn't sound very sure, but it was the only thing we had. Seconds later, my phone rang with Marco's name and face scrolling the screen.

"Shit," I mumbled before answering. "Marco! What's going—"

"Have you seen Bender?! Oh my God, Ioan. What the fuck is going on? Where did they get that picture? Now I'm seeing it on Twitter, Instagram...Jesus Christ Ioan!" he yelled in my ear and I had to hold the phone away from my head. "Has Ezra seen this? Billy? Jesus Christ!"

"Marco!" I snapped back. "Listen to me, this is...well, I'm not sure what it is."

I looked to Alyssa for guidance, but she gave me a thoughtful look. "Put it on speaker," she mouthed.

I frowned at her.

"Do it," she mouthed again, so I did.

"Ioan...you guys almost have your album finished...why are you letting this woman get in the way? Mikal says you won't sign the contract. You're holding the rest of the guys hostage playing these games!" he was barking as Alyssa and I listened.

Frustrated, I could only roll my eyes and let him continue.

"Boy, I'm telling you," he barely took a breath, and I imagined his Northern Italian face becoming scarlet, "Get this shit under control. Get her out of your house. Sign that goddamn contract."

Lys' eyes bulged in her head, and I had to look away from her. She didn't understand that this was normal in my business. Managers and executives get pissed off and push artists around. This wasn't the first time Marco blew his top, and it definitely wouldn't be the last.

"Are you finished?" I asked calmly. I heard a huff of breath on the line.

"What?!" he roared.

"Marco, Lyssie has nothing to do with any of this...but someone is trying to make her into the bad guy." I paused. "The guys and I aren't breaking up...that's ridiculous. And as far as Mikal is concerned...I haven't signed the contract because I want to make sure we're getting a fair cut."

"Mikal has been nothing but fair—"

But it was my turn to cut him off, "No, Marco, he hasn't. Did you even read the contract? He wants his name attached to every song as a producer and to receive creative credit. Furthermore, he has an addendum that states the label gets a larger cut of every song his name is on...and it's more than what any of us get. It's bullshit! He got his panties in a knot because we wanted Delmonico on this album instead of him, and now, he's tightening the screws."

The line was quiet for a long moment and I thought the call had dropped.

"Marco?"

"Yeah, I'm here. I'll talk to Mikal...see what I can do," he conceded, albeit reluctantly.

"You do that," I replied and abruptly hung up. Feeling Lys' stare on me, I glanced in her direction. "I'm sorry about that."

Her hazel eyes considered me for a long moment. "First, you owe no one, especially me, an apology. Second," another pause. "Where is this contract?"

I frowned, "Uhhh, I think in the back of the car where I left it the other day."

"Get it," she ordered and I saw the wheels in her head turning.

"Alyssa, it's a contract. I'll have the corporate lawyer look over it...Mikal and I will negotiate conditions and we'll be done. It's not a big deal," I said.

Her smile was soft, "Ioan. I need you to trust me...please. Get me the contract."

Chapter Thirty-One

Alyssa

I sat cross-legged on the sofa surrounded by pages of legalese and breakfast dishes. Scowling at Ioan, I grumbled under my breath as I tried to sort and reassemble the scattered paperwork in the correct order. I had a hunch there was something in there Marco desperately wanted Ioan to sign off on. Was he trying to get a larger cut of the pie?

Then again, there was Tessie. What were the odds that she was at the same shows that Ioan's stalker happened to follow him to? I couldn't believe it was a coincidence. There wasn't a high roller in all of Sin City who would take that gamble.

"Okay," I said with confidence. "We're in business."

I started skimming the documents, but the first few pages were standard introductions. I quickly realized I wasn't the person who needed to have their eyes on this document. Picking up my phone, I dialed Bett's number.

"I'm at your service, my Queen," her chipper voice rang as a hello. "What does her royal highness command?"

Chuckling, I smiled, "I'm going to send you a contract. I need the Cliff Notes edition."

"Of course, my liege," I heard her tapping frenetic keystrokes. "Length of said document?"

"Best guess?" I mused, "Around four-hundred."

Bett choked, and I heard her teacup clatter, "Did you say four-hun-dred pages?"

"Yeah," I shrugged as if she could see me.

"Uhhmmm, okay. That's going to take me at least," she hummed as she took her moment. "Give me a day, probably two. Elf-warrior Bett, out."

She hung up the phone. Using the scanner in Ioan's office, I sent the entire file to Bett with a note telling her to call me as soon as she had anything. Returning to the living room, I found Ioan pacing.

"What's wrong?" I asked.

He shook his head, "Just...anxious."

He crossed the space between us in three large strides, pulling me into his hold. He ran a trail of kisses down my neck, and my skin vibrated, but we had to be careful.

"Ioan," I stopped him. "The shades are open."

"So?" he pulled away. "We're supposed to be putting on a show for the stalker, right? Let's give them a good one."

His cheek pulled into that arrogant grin, the one that made my knees weak. "My *team* might be watching, Ioan. And besides, aren't we supposed to be leaving for a party at Ezra's soon?"

Ioan groaned, "Yes."

"Well, then, march your ass upstairs, sir. And put on your party clothes," I smacked him on the butt.

By five-thirty, we were in the car heading into Los Angeles proper to attend the sixth birthday party of Ezra's son, Sean. I turned in the seat to make sure the gifts we purchased and wrapped were tucked in safely as Ioan entered the freeway.

Sitting back in my seat, I thought of Daisy, and my heart missed her so much. Saying good morning and goodnight to her at the beginning and end of my day just wasn't enough. I knew when I signed on for this assignment, it could take a while, but in just a few days, I will have been without my daughter for a month, and it killed me.

So much had happened in the last few weeks, and I wanted, no, needed, to feel her tiny hand on my cheek and nuzzle into her strawberry-scented hair. She was having the best time with Kate, but it was the way she said *'Mommy, when will you be home?'* every night that left my soul empty because I didn't have an answer.

I felt the sting of tears pierce my eyes and I shifted to look out the window. I had to swallow down those emotions and put them aside. I wouldn't let Ioan see me crying again.

"So," I swallowed the slowly diminishing lump in my throat, "How many kids do Ezra and Val have again?"

A bright smile spread across his lips, "Three. All boys...and all completely different."

I saw the pride on his face. He seemed to be very taken by his adoptive nephews. It made me wonder if, at the end of all of this, he wanted to settle down and have his own family. Aside from a dark room, there weren't many things that scared me, but that was a thought that sent a chill of fear to my bones. I was already a mom, and Daisy held all of my heart, but the thought of being anyone's vessel of domesticity made me want to vomit.

I would admit that was probably over dramatic, but I had my reasons; namely, my worthless parents, Trish and John Salerno. My therapist told me that it was up to me to break the cycle of abuse, and I thought long and hard on those words for years, deciding a long time ago that their lineage would end with me. Whatever nonsense was in my DNA, I wouldn't ever pass it to another innocent human. I wanted their legacy, for whatever it was worth, to be erased.

My life changed the first night I stood watch over a tiny little girl in the burn unit at University Medical Center. My assignment was to make sure the foster parents didn't sneak onto the floor and snatch her while the authorities waited for court and restraining orders. I was only supposed to be there for the night, but I stayed a week. Not because she was in danger, but because she was mine. In my duty to her I found a piece of my heart that was missing and when she woke on night five from a nightmare, or, maybe it was pain, her small arms wrapped around my neck and she uttered through sobs, "Ma-ma".

Her desperate cry ripped my soul and she ended the old me and the new me was her mom.

But, through all the fight it took for her to legally be mine, the heartache, the worry, and the unconditional love, I held true to my original belief; I would not allow my past, my parents poison to eek its festering contagion into this world again. Daisy was my child, I didn't have to give birth to her for that to be true and she would be a better human for it.

Ioan's fingers moved over my hand softly, "You okay?"

"Yeah," I smiled weakly, shaking the internal monologue from my head. "Just figuring things out."

I noticed we were stopped. I looked through the window at a modestly large home of white stucco set back from the street. "Oh! We're here."

"Yup. For a few minutes."

I also realized the car wasn't running. Pursing my lips, I gave Ioan a side glance, "You were just going to see how long it took me to notice, weren't you?"

The space in the car crackled with laughter as he opened his door.

Chapter Thirty-Two

Alyssa

"Come in!" Val moved just behind the large oak door for us to pass. Ioan leaned into her, kissing her cheek. "Please excuse the noise and the mess...Sean had a sleep over last night and they've all been running wild since eight this morning."

A cacophony of squeals and pounding feet across the floor echoed off the marble tile of the foyer. A lanky boy with sandy hair tore around the corner and flung himself at Ioan. He barely had time to catch him before the child threw his hands around Ioan's neck and hung there.

"Sean Ezra!" Val scolded her son.

Ioan let out a howl of laughter, "C'mon, Val...he's fine." He gave the boy a tight hug, "Hey, kiddo, happy birthday!"

"Thanks, Uncle Yo! Wanna see my new trampoline?" Sean's bright eyes beamed.

Ioan smiled, "Uhh..yeah! Where's your pops?"

"He's changing Sawyer's poopy pants," he giggled, squeezing Ioan's nose before pulling on his earlobes playfully. He turned his bright blue eyes on me, "Who is she?"

"This is my friend, Lyssie."

"Ooooo...is she your *girlfriend*?" he teased.

Ioan's face blushed, "Maybe. What's it to you, punk? Trying to steal my girl?" With a fast movement, he flipped Sean over, hanging the skinny child by his ankles, and the boy shrieked with delight.

"Swing me, Uncle Yo!"

"Oookay. Sean...go back outside and take Summit with you," Val gave a tired laugh. Ioan gently placed him back on the ground and tousled his hair when he stood.

"Yeah, *Sean Ezra*," he mocked.

I watched Sean dart into the living room, pick up the hand of another younger boy with bright red hair, and pull him out a set of French doors at the back of the room. We all stood for a small moment, taking in all the energy that just exited the space. Val's sigh of relief cut our brief silence.

"All that since eight?" Ioan laughed.

"Uh huh." She rolled her eyes, "Come on back to the den...my parents will be here shortly. Can I get you guys something to drink?"

After a quick detour through the kitchen for lemonade, the three of us entered an enormous living space with two plush sofas and what had to be a ninety-eight-inch television playing cartoons mounted over a grand fireplace. Ezra sat shirtless and cross-legged in the corner of one of the sectionals, bouncing who I could only assume was Sawyer, the third Stanley boy. Ioan strode behind his friend, clasping him on the shoulder. Leaning down, his eyes widened as he cooed at the toddler. "Hey little man...what's going on?"

"Tell Uncle Yo you're almost a man...at least you shit like one," Ezra laughed and handed the freshly diapered baby over his head to Ioan. "Hold him, I've got to put on a shirt."

Val stepped forward, "Want me to take him?"

"Nah," Ioan jostled the baby around to cradle him on his hip. "I've got him."

Taking a seat next to me, he bounced the chubby boy on his leg as the child smiled unabashedly at me with a large, four-tooth grin. His deep blue eyes were identical to his eldest brother's, but unlike Sean and what I saw of Summit, Sawyer had dark, almost black hair.

"He's adorable," I chirped to Val, and she smiled.

"Thanks! I think so too."

I caressed his meaty hand between my fingers, "How old is he?"

"Thirteen months," she chuckled. "Do you have children?"

My heart skipped a beat, but I was able to compose myself quickly. I hadn't expected the question and I didn't know how much Ezra had told his wife about what was really going on. Regardless, I didn't want to discuss my real life, my private life, outside of Ioan.

"No, I don't," I replied and felt Ioan's deep eyes bore down on me. I wasn't about to turn to him and react to his stare. I was grateful when Ezra returned fully clothed and with his own beverage.

"Babe, I think your parents are here," he said to Val. "I'll get the dogs on the grill in just a minute."

She jumped from her seat, reaching her hands out to the baby, "C'mon kiddo...let's get you some one-on-one time with Grammy and Gramps before your brothers fight for all the attention."

As Val left the room, I watched Ezra's eyes follow her out into the hallway leading to the front door. When he was sure she was out of earshot, he sat next to Ioan on the sofa.

He leaned forward, "So, are you any closer to finding out who this crazy person is?"

"We're narrowing down the suspect pool," I sighed.

It wasn't a total lie; the suspect list was pretty short, it was just a matter of putting the pieces together.

"What does your wife know?" I asked pointedly. For as close as the three of them seemed to be, I found it odd that she had yet to mention anything about what was going on.

Ezra shook his head, "Nothing. She has enough to deal with chasing after three boys and us being out of town for months at a time. I wasn't about to worry her with some damn stalker. Especially now."

I nodded, but Ioan cut in, narrowing his eyes on his friend, "What do you mean by that?"

Ezra chewed on the inside of his lip, "Val's pregnant again."

"What!? Are you serious?" Ioan blurted loudly.

I sank back into the overstuffed cushions of the sofa. This wasn't a conversation for me and I did my best to melt away.

"Shhhh!" Ezra put a finger to his lips before lowering his voice. "We just found out a couple days ago. Val's a little freaked out because Sawyers' not that old. We really were hoping our next would be spaced a little more, but I guess it is what it is."

"Dude," Ioan's grin enveloped his entire face. "That's so cool. I'm gonna get another nephew."

Ezra laughed, "Hopefully not. The balance in this house is already way off...I'm crossing my fingers for a girl." His voice dropped again, "That's why I haven't said anything to her yet. I need her focused on what she and the new baby needs...not worrying about anything else." He paused. "And don't tell her you know. She'll kill me."

"I got you, Pops," Ioan clapped his hand on Ezra's back.

"Thanks," he chuckled. "I better get the food started. There are four boys outside that are about an hour from becoming feral."

Ioan lifted his glass, "I'll be out in a minute to help." He waited until Ezra was gone before turning his entire body in my direction. His eyes searched my face as if he was trying to read me. "Why did you lie to Val?"

Damn it. I knew he'd call me out for that.

"We've been through this. I keep my private life closed—"

"Alyssa, this is my family. You can trust them," he replied. "What happens at the end of this? Huh? What do we tell her when you catch this person and we can be a normal couple? *'Sorry I lied...please don't think it's because I thought you were a suspect?'*"

His dark eyes pleaded with me for answers, but before I could formulate a cohesive thought, something deep in my brain triggered my mouth to move without reason and the words spilled out of me.

"Do you want to have kids of your own?"

He blinked with confusion, "What?"

My mind screamed for me to shut up, but the voice that was growing all day somewhere deep in my subconscious won out, "Do you want to settle down and have your own kids? Like Ezra and Val?"

Jesus Alyssa. Shut. The. Fuck. Up.

"Uhmmm," his eyes looked nearly panicked. "Alyssa, this isn't the conversation we should be having. Not here."

"But it is. This is the exact conversation," I stated as a matter of fact. I had already dug the hole; might as well bury myself in it. "I don't. I don't want to have any kids...from me. I have Daisy...and if I want to give her a sibling, I don't want that child coming from me."

Ioan stared at me for a long time. I thought maybe he didn't hear me or that this would be a deal breaker for him. Was I reading too much into it? Did I just make a complete ass of myself? The answer to that question was a resounding yes, but it was too late. I couldn't un-ring the bell.

We heard commotion coming from just off the den and realized Val and her parents were heading our way. He scooted closer to me, his voice barely above a whisper, "We can have this conversation, just not here." His eyes searched my face and it felt a little like pity, which I absolutely hated. Before I could open my mouth again, he continued, "I'll have an answer for you, just give me time to process."

At that moment, the room filled with grandparents and kids and all manner of wild sounds. The party was underway and I was swept into its festivities. But the annoying little monster in the back of my mind replayed his answer over and over.

'Just give me time to process.'

In my mind, that could only mean one thing: that if we stayed together, he would be giving up something he wanted, and I couldn't have that. I cared too much about him to deprive him of anything. If a family of his own was what he wanted, then he could have that, and I wouldn't stop him; I just couldn't be the one to give it to him. I would have to let him go.

One invasive thought led to the next: Would I be strong enough to do it?

"Lyssie? You okay?" Val's voice cut through my tunnel vision. I looked down at what I was doing only to realize the tomato I had been slicing was well past the stem and I held the knife dangerously close to my fingers.

"Oh, yeah...I'm great!" I blinked, lowering the blade from my hand.

Val's steely eyes narrowed, "You were off in lala land. But I get it."

"Get...what?" I asked.

She nodded in the direction of the French doors leading to the backyard. Not three feet beyond them, Ioan and Ezra stood next to a large gas grill loaded with hot dogs and burgers. We could hear the muffled sounds of laughter as the men talked gregariously to Val's father, Jim.

"If you're wondering if Ioan feels the same way, he does. I haven't seen him this relaxed or...happy in, well, ever," she smiled.

I felt heat rising in my cheeks, "Oh."

Val gave me a grin that was warm and reassuring, "Any doubts you're having, don't. Ioan is a really good guy. And he must care about you a lot because he's never brought a woman over when the boys were here."

"Thanks," I replied.

We finished cutting the vegetables and preparing the sides just as Ezra waved to us, letting us know the food was ready. After dinner, there was cake and ice cream for the birthday boy and presents. Sean was super excited when he unwrapped the two large boxes from Ioan and me.

After lots of discussion about what was appropriate for a six-year-old and the consequences to his parents, we settled on an arcade-style basketball hoop game. He howled with delight and begged Ioan, his dad, and grandpa to put it together so they could play. And of course, he got what he wanted.

After Val's parents left around ten o'clock, Val put little Sawyer down in his bed as Ezra wrestled the red-headed energy bomb that was Summit into pajamas with cartoon puppies on them. His friends long since gone, Sean finally settled into the corner of one of the sofas and fell asleep somewhere around eleven.

The four of us chatted for a while longer but I couldn't really concentrate on any of the conversation. The closer we got to leaving, the higher my anxiety went. I wanted desperately to take this day back. I should've clamped down on my tongue before I'd made such a complete ass of myself in front of Ioan. I had no right to corner him like I did. All he wanted was to bring me into his family, and I freaked out and made it about something completely different.

There would be consequences, and I knew I wouldn't like the fallout.

Chapter
Thirty-Three

Ioan

I t was around midnight when I eased off of Chaparal heading to the four-oh-five. Ezra and Alyssa gave me a lot to think about today and all I wanted to do was crank up the music and drive. It was bad enough that Alyssa had come from so far out in left field with her starting a family question, but only got worse when Ezra cornered me the second I got outside to help at the grill.

"So, you and assassin girl, huh?"

I nearly spit my lemonade.

"Uhhhmm...no...I mean, it's all an act," I lied. From the look on Ezra's face, and the absolutely raucous, and almost insulting laughter emanating from his chest, he saw right through me.

"Yeahhh...okay," he patronized me. "Who the fuck do you think you're talking to?"

My best friend of too many years to count. Ezra and I grew up in the same neighborhood, on the same block, on the outskirts of Chicago. As kids, we were nearly inseparable and still were. He was the first person to come see me when I was in the hospital after the fire and it was his parents that took me in when I had nowhere to go. I sighed and couldn't stop my face when it pulled into a goofy, lovesick grin.

"Oh, God. How bad do you have it for her?" he huffed out another chuckle. "Is she into you?"

I pursed my mouth, my head bobbing as I tried to pick the right words from thin air. I was doing an awful job of maintaining my chill.

Ezra stared at me, wide-eyed, then sat his glass down on the edge of the prep table, "Shiiit. You fucked her, didn't you?"

I frowned at his choice of word. With anyone else, I wouldn't have cared, but when it came to Alyssa, it sounded crass. "Have we had sex? Yes."

"Jesus fucking Christ! Isn't that against the rules or something? Like, a conflict of interest?" Ezra's eyes sharpened on me before tossing hotdogs on the hot surface. "How much do you know about her?"

I know he was trying to protect me. It was something we had done for each other over the years. When life on the road got too wild, we'd keep each other accountable. Ezra thought I was going way, way off the farm.

"Ez...stop. This isn't like that...not like it was back in the day when we were pulling girls off our bus. I really, really care about her...and yes, she feels the same way. We have something here, Ez. And it's like nothing I've ever had before." I paused but the look on his face told me he wasn't convinced. "Do you remember the first night you met Val? You told me you knew from the second you saw her she was the one."

He nodded.

"I knew it a year ago, and I'm sure now...she's mine. Ez, she's smart, and strong and—" I wanted to go on and on about all the things Alyssa was, but Ezra cut me off.

"Hot?"

I wanted to punch him as I broke into laughter, "Yeah, she's that too."

"How much does she know?" he rolled the hot dogs over the grates of the grill with a pair of tongs and didn't have to elaborate. I knew what he meant.

"Everything. Completely exposed," I replied.

He concentrated on the task in front of him for a long moment, "How did she get into being a...bodyguard...assassin...mercenary?"

I chuckled, "She's not most of those things, you know."

He smiled as his shoulders lifted and fell in a shrug.

"Her childhood was more fucked up than mine, honestly. This job saved her," I explained. I moved closer to the grill taking the spatula off the rack. This guy was going to burn the burgers if he wasn't careful.

Ezra watched me flip the charred patties and finished his drink, "So. You're into a hot, dangerous, complicated woman who could probably kill you fifteen different ways. Who knew my best friend had that particular kink?"

He wasn't wrong. The fact that she could handle herself and carried a gun was a turn on.

"You need to find out for sure if she loves you as much as you clearly do her," he started pulling food off the grill. "Make sure you're both on the same page."

We were, that I was sure of...weren't we? I remembered Alyssa's left field questions. I knew she wanted an answer, and I had one to give, but it terrified me because I had never said it out loud. I was lost in those thoughts as I merged onto the freeway and a motorcycle buzzed by at lightning speed.

Alyssa sat a little straighter, "Jesus. Someone's in a hurry."

"Idiot," I mumbled under my breath.

The traffic was most always heavy in LA, especially in the day, and at night, while still busy, wasn't the vehicular overload that you find at rush hour. Just as I approached the Wilshire exit, a single bright light reflected off my rearview mirror, hitting me directly in the eyes. I swore and cursed LEDS as the car was fully illuminated. The high pitch of a motorcycle whirred as the light moved around to my side of the car and kept pace. Alyssa's head bobbed around me to see out the windows.

"Ioan...drive faster," her voice was calm and commanding.

"What? Why?"

"I need you to do as I say." She pulled out her cell phone and hit one button. "That's the same bike. Do whatever you need to do to keep ahead."

I nodded and pressed the accelerator harder, pulling away from our pursuer.

"Fox, we're on the four-oh-five south heading back to Ioan's. The tail is operating what could be a Yamaha R-1...too dark for color." Her voice tense as she turned in her seat, keeping an eye on the bike.

"How the hell do you know that?" I asked incredulously.

Holding the phone away from her mouth, she replied, "I like motorcycles." She paused, "Ioan, faster, please."

Pressing the pedal nearly to the floor, I looked at my dashboard. I was going nearly one hundred miles per hour, and this fuck was still up my ass.

"Do not take the exit!" She ordered. "Fox, how far are you?"

Another pause.

"Where do we go, Fox?"

Her voice sounded a little desperate, which pissed me off. Who did this asshole think he was? If this turned out to be a paparazzi, I would own whatever rag he was from.

"Hang on!" I bellowed and laid the accelerator to the floor. The car shot through the nearly empty lane like a bullet.

"Ioan! What are you doing?" Alyssa screamed and grasped for her seatbelt.

"Getting us the fuck out of here," I growled. "Tell him we're headed for Del Rey Beach."

Alyssa disconnected the call, "The team will meet us there. *If* we get there in one piece."

She squirmed in her seat as I veered around cars, chasing our exit. But I had to admit, my Mercedes was no match for the smaller and more maneuverable bike. I bounced from lane to lane, putting as many obstacles between them and us until I saw the exit up ahead. It was then that I realized what I was doing was counterproductive so I shifted quickly into the carpool lane, bringing my speed down just a bit.

"Uhhh...Ioan, what are you doing?" Alyssa grasped the dash before turning her eyes back on the motorcycle. "Ioan! He's got a gun...we need to get out of here!"

I saw my opening and took it. After I saw him, gun drawn at the back driver's panel, I jerked the wheel, crossed the four lanes, and raced down the off ramp.

And right into a line of traffic.

"Fuck!" I snarled before hopping a curb to turn down a side street that was nearly clear.

I drove faster through the narrow street. Hearing Alyssa sucking in a deep breath, I imagined she was holding it as she talked herself down, all to avoid climbing the edges of the car. Unexpectedly, and to my utter surprise, she put her hand on my thigh. My muscles instinctually twitched in response, but I had to admit the warmth it gave was comforting.

She shifted again in her seat looking outside the car in all directions, "I don't see him...might be nice if you'd slow down."

Chapter Thirty-Four

Alyssa

I was sure I would die in that car.

Setting his foot harder on the gas, horns blared around us as Ioan switched lanes in drastic fashion and turned down city streets that became more narrow. I grasped his free hand and his fingers curled around mine. Electricity shot through my entire body and my heart pounded; not because I was still afraid of dying with his driving, but because I loved the way his hand felt.

Protective and sure.

His dark eyes showed genuine concern, "I won't let anything happen to you...you're safe."

"I'd feel safer if we weren't on this road in this car. I don't like this kind of traffic," I admitted. "Or playing Indy Five Hundred."

Ioan squeezed my hand on my thigh. Fire shot through me and singed my nerve endings.

What was he doing? This wasn't the time or the place.

A few more turns and I saw through the dusky haze of streetlamps the Pacific appear on the horizon. Pulling alongside the sidewalk, Ioan's cocky grin started to appear but faded just as quickly when he saw the look of horror on my face. His eyes softened like I'd never seen them before and he held on to my hand. It was like magnets being drawn together as we leaned closer in our seats. Half of me wanted to laugh nervously in his face because I was glad to be alive. But the other half....

Our mouths came together and an explosion of volcanic power erupted in my soul.

When we pulled away, I watched a dark cloud roll over his eyes; it was a shadow of worry and it gave me pause. "What's wrong?"

He shook his head, "Are you okay?"

"Yeah," I nodded.

"Are you sure?" his large hand stroked my face.

A smiled pulled at my cheeks, "Well, your driving could use some practice, but other than that—"

My thought was interrupted when Ioan pulled my face toward his, gently resting his lips on mine. After a moment, he sat back in his seat, staring at me. Our eyes were locked for a long minute before we noticed a black suburban skid to a stop several feet behind us.

"Can we pick this up later?" he whispered.

I nodded.

In my sideview mirror, I watched Fox and Chico jump from the vehicle, guns drawn taking careful steps toward us. I rolled down the window, "We're all good!"

As we exited the car, the guys holstered their weapons, looking satisfied. I knew the tracking device we placed on both of Ioan's vehicles could be a potential asset, I just didn't realize we would have to put it to a real world application. Regardless, I felt better knowing it worked and the team found us easily.

"Gotta say," Fox smiled, "Impressive driving for a musician."

Ioan frowned playfully, "That almost sounds like a compliment."

"Hmmm, you would think so, huh?" I eyed my partner.

"I'm serious," Fox countered. "Slick move on the freeway...pulling that guy in, then losing him at the ramp. Smart."

Ioan shrugged.

"Did she scream?" he asked and I glared at him.

Ioan looked from me to Fox then to Chico, "Did who scream?"

Fox's eyes rolled as he pointed at me, "Her. Let's just say Lys doesn't do traffic well."

"No, she never said a word. Well, unless that warning about a gun is considered screaming...but I don't think so," Ioan's head shook as he lied through his teeth to my partner.

Fox's jaw dropped in disbelief, "Nah...no way. We saw everything on the drone...no way she made it through without some white knuckles."

"You owe me ten bucks," Chico laughed. "Pay up, rich boy."

Fox dug in his pocket, pulling out a small, silver money clip and unfurled several bills. He shoved a ten spot at Chico and he smiled broadly.

I sighed, "I hate to break up all this fun at my expense, but did Bett get any good pictures from the drone yet?"

Chico shook his head as he placed the money in the front pocket of his dark jeans, "No...everything was moving too fast and it was dark. We've already got Quen's team back at the house and no sign of the driver. Bett will keep at it and let us know if she finds anything."

"We'll follow you back," Fox said.

We were all back on the freeway heading for Ioan's in Santa Monica within minutes. The drive back was quiet and before I realized, thirty minutes had passed and he was entering the passcode on the gate. He parked the car in the garage before we got out and entered through a secondary side door and breezeway. I looked around at our surroundings.

"What are you doing?" he asked, his first words spoken to me in almost an hour were husky and drawn.

"Nothing...I guess I didn't notice when the guys dropped away," I admitted.

"Oh," Ioan punched in his code to the door. "About five minutes before we hit the drive. You sure you're okay?"

Following him into the large laundry room, I nodded in the dark, "Yeah, I've just had something on my mind since we left."

"Yeah, what's that?" he asked and felt for the light.

I couldn't actually tell him. But if he was going to say he couldn't live without a family of his own, then this would probably be my last night with him and I needed to feel him one more time. Taking his hand, I pulled him around to face me. I wrapped my hand in this shirts' collar and tugged hard, forcing him to bend in my direction. Throwing my free arm around his neck, I pressed my lips to his and let our mouths dance.

Ioan wrapped his body around mine, drawing me in before lifting me from the floor and plopping me on a table next to the washing machine. My hands yanked at his shirt tucked into his pants and I pulled it over his head. Our movements were frenetic as we both anticipated what the other would do next.

He pulled my hips into his and I laid soft pecks along his chest until I came to his nipple. My teeth made contact and I left a small nibble behind. Ioan hissed with pleasure.

"Do it again," he snarled. "And don't stop."

I did but this time I dug my teeth in harder sucking at his skin before I pulled away. I felt his length harden on my inner thigh and I tore at the button on his jeans to free him. Once they were unzipped, I wrapped my legs around his hips and pushed his pants down with my feet.

His dark eyes glinted in the dim light from the breezeway as his completely naked self stared down at me. I watched his broad chest rise and fall in a heavy panting rhythm.

"You're a little overdressed," his voice raspy.

My heart thudded just beneath my chest, "Maybe we should fix that."

Ioan's hands slid beneath my t-shirt bringing it and my bra over my head before sliding his fingers between my waist and my skirt, pulling them to the floor. The table was cold on my bare ass but I barely felt it as a rush of heat rose in my core. He leaned into me, his warm hands cradling my back. Grabbing a thick blanket folded on the dryer, I threw it on the ground over our clothes as his tongue traced my collar bone.

"Get on the floor," I ordered softly in his ear, then bit his lobe. The growling sound he purred made my center slick.

Ioan picked me off the table, his sultry eyes never leaving mine and we slowly slid to the blanket. As he tried to pull me under him, I pushed his shoulders with both hands and he fell back. "No," I smiled deviously.

Straddling his hips, I lined my entrance to him and Ioan, realizing what I was doing, grasped my hips tightly and drove his cock into me.

"Oh my God!" The words rumbled from somewhere deep inside him.

I ground into him, stroking every inch of his length with my core. With every rock of my body, he pushed deeper, filling me with every-thing he had. I loved the feeling of Ioan Johns. The way my skin tingled when his skin touched mine. The taste of him on my lips. The smell of his cologne. The strength in those beautifully tattooed arms. I knew I would never have enough.

Leaning into his chest, I bit his shoulder and he cried out, "Alyssa! God woman...you don't know what you're doing to me."

But I did know. I pieced together exactly what drove him to unfet-tered delight.

His fingers dug into my ass as he lifted me with his pelvis off the floor. If he were practicing yoga, it would have been a perfect bridge pose, but this was something otherworldly as his cock pressed deep against my walls. I called out his name, and he lowered me slowly back down.

"Again!" I commanded. I wanted him as far inside me as he could go. This was my pain and pleasure moment. Ioan was a large man in every way, and I wanted to take all of him in, especially if this was my last chance.

Lifting me again, I continued to take his length in a steady rhythm, stroking him with every bounce of my hips. My nails scraped down his chest as I fought the urge to quicken my pace. I wanted this to last forever. As Ioan brought me back to the floor, he released my hips, found my swollen clit, and worked it between his fingers softly.

I came undone.

Rivers flowed, and my core tightened in rhythmic spasms around his cock. Ioan groaned, "Oh yeah...that's it *Alyssa...*"

My name from his lips sounded like lyrics from one of his songs.

I felt the waves of orgasm build at the base of my spine and fall over me like a rip tide. My center clenched around him, drawing him deeper as he thrust into me. Stars burst behind my eyes as I fought the urge to close them and delight in every sensation this man gave.

"Alyss-a!" he bellowed as I felt him flood me.

Our climax was hard and frenetic until I collapsed to his side, on the cool blanket, panting and sweating. Ioan pulled me tight, his strong arms holding me against his chest. It took us several minutes to catch our breath, and in those moments, I listened to every beat of his heart.

He stroked my face with his finger, "A penny for your thoughts?"

"That's all their worth?" I giggled.

Ioan laughed, "Well, what's your counteroffer?"

My mouth gaped, and I shot him a look of playful offense, "If you're going to be that way, I'd say they're out of your price range now."

"Name it, Salerno," his fingers tickled my side and I erupted in squeals which triggered a wrestling match that I lost, on purpose. It was in this abating laughter that our eyes met again. I found comfort and completion in his smokey stare and it was a feeling that was wholly unfamiliar.

And scared the shit out of me too.

But I allowed it to sink under my skin and into my bones; to become part of me and like oxygen it was something I couldn't live without. It was also something I didn't think I would be able to tell him even if I lived a thousand years. Ioan cleared his throat.

"I would give you every dollar I have...every piece of music I've ever written...every beat of my heart to know what runs through that beautiful mind of yours," he whispered.

My breath shuttered and Ioan raised up, propping himself on an elbow. "Can we talk about today?"

I was never so glad for the dark as I was then. I was honestly surprised my embarrassment didn't shine like a glowstick at a rave. In my effort to feel every part of him on my skin, I had almost forgotten about my giant mouth and its revolt from reason.

"Look...I'm sorry—"

"Wait a minute," he stopped me. "You don't have anything to apologize for...I understand."

"Understand, what, exactly?"

He hooked his finger under my chin, "The reason why you don't want children of your own. I get it."

"Do you?" I pressed because I would be utterly speechless if he did. Part of me expected the next thing out of his mouth would be something about reconsideration or finding the right partner. That would be it; the breaking point. I would have to walk away.

"I don't want," he paused. And in the dim light from the back stoop, I saw his eyes narrow in concentration. He was struggling with his next words. "I've never worried about becoming my father. And even though I know his violence probably isn't something that can be passed down...part of me still wonders what if. What if there was something *wrong* with him...you know? I can't live with that."

I inhaled slowly and held it. "What are you saying?"

"That I understand. And that I support your decision, because with it, you're supporting mine," he whispered.

The last thin shield that surrounded my heart shattered, and I fell into him. There were no barriers between us anymore. I belonged to Ioan Johns, and Ioan Johns belonged to me.

Chapter Thirty-Five

Ioan

S tretching my arms across the bed, I realized I was alone. For a split second, in the haze of waking, the thought crossed my mind that everything that happened last night and every night prior was a dream. I ran my hands over my head and down my chest and I felt it. A small tender spot on the edge of my nipple. A sweet reminder of a night spent with Alyssa.

After a quick shower, I found her sitting cross legged on the sofa sipping cold coffee through a straw. An Air Pod in one ear and smiling brightly into her phone. A call that I could only assume was with Daisy. Not being someone who eavesdrops, I went to the kitchen to grind beans for an espresso. Coffee in hand, I leaned against the bar checking email on my phone when Alyssa's voice called from the other room.

"You can come in here, you know."

Sauntering through the doorway, I smiled, "I didn't want to interrupt." I leaned in and kissed her softly, "You're up early."

"Early meeting with Bett," she replied. "Then my wake-up call to Daisy."

I raised my eyebrows, "What did she say?"

"That she wants to go swimming today and that she doesn't think all fairies have wings," she took another pull of coffee through her grin.

I tilted my head, "Uhh...I'm pretty sure they do. Wouldn't a fairy without wings be a pixie?" Alyssa nearly choked on her coffee in laughter, but I continued, "I was actually wondering about what Bett had to say."

"Not much. Unfortunately, Chico was right...it was too dark to get any sort of ID on the driver or the bike," she sighed.

"What do we do now?" I asked.

She shrugged, "I keep working the clues. They're going to slip up...Fox almost had them last night."

"Did she mention the contract?" I hesitated asking, because I knew as soon as Alyssa's genius computer whiz knew anything, we would as well.

"Still sifting through it," she frowned. "She should have a handle on it by tonight.

My hand ran involuntarily over my chest, just barely touching the spot where I was bruised from Alyssa's bite. I wanted to be more angry that someone took another shot at me, but now it was feeling like second nature. My next immediate thought was about her. Last night it wasn't just me in danger, but Alyssa too. That was all I needed for the fury to rise.

The more I thought about the last several weeks, the more I realized she was in just as much danger *because* of me. I wasn't an investigator like Alyssa; or a cop, or anything like that. I was a guy with a voice in a rock band. But, I was also the man who would burn the world down if anything happened to her. Not wanting her to see the absolute maddening rage storming inside me, I turned away from her and walked to the front door.

"Where are you going?" She called after me.

"Morning paper," I growled to myself. I worked myself up into such a mood that I didn't hear what else she said to me. I flung the door open and marched with angry purpose to the slot in my stone wall where I had the Times and all the other tabloid rags delivered. Could I find all of these things online? Absolutely, but again, there was just something about holding the physical copy in my hand. When I pulled on the small closure though, the box was empty.

Perfect.

I turned back, returning to my front door, only to find myself walking a little slower. I had to calm down before I reentered the house because I refused to ruin a beautiful Sunday with the amazing woman inside. I worked to get my mind off the night before as best as I could. But, it wasn't all bad, was it? After we arrived home, the night took a delicious turn and even now, memories of the sensation of her wrapped around me made me hard, again.

I fought the urge to run inside, carry her over my shoulder to my bed and keep her naked all day. Caveman style. That's the way I wanted to spend a Sunday afternoon; locked in my bedroom doing lewd and unspeakable things with Alyssa. Right now it was impossible; we had roles to play in this game of cat and mouse. Alyssa's head always seemed to be laser focused on nothing but the game during the daylight; when others could see.

Maybe it was impatience I felt. While this all started as a ruse to lure out some mentally-unstable fan, I had fallen in love with the woman planted in my home and I was sick of hiding it from everyone. Clearly, Ezra knew, but he knew me better than I did myself most of the time. But no one else. Sure, the rest of the band, Marco, and even Mikal thought we were a happy little couple, but none of that was real and I wanted to declare it to the world. Our world.

Then I considered the members of her team. I didn't know exactly how close she was to any of them, other than Jake, so I wasn't sure if she had confided in them. Maybe there were rules against it? Maybe Ezra was right and it was a conflict of interest, or something? Regardless, I want them to know too. I needed everyone important to us to know she was everything I ever dreamed about.

As I stepped onto the stoop, I heard a distinctive sound of huffing breath as I ran right into Alyssa.

"Oh my God, I'm so sorry!" Catching her by the shoulders I steadied her before she toppled sideways.

She latched on my forearms for balance, "Didn't you hear me?"

I shook my head, "Sorry...got lost in my head."

"I already pulled the papers from the box, they're inside on the bar," she laced her fingers with mine, pulling me inside.

Returning to the coffee machine, I made my second and final cup of the morning before settling down on one of the stools to flip through the rags. It had been about a week since the previous headline referencing either of us, so I was already a little apprehensive. First one down and nothing. But as I turned the cover over on the second, the small cup I held in my right hand clattered to the marble counter.

I saw nothing but red.

Chapter Thirty-Six

Alyssa

"Good morning, Wheels. Oh, I mean, Mr. Merritt," I stifled a small laugh as I answered my cell.

"Lys," over the line, Jake's voice was already serious and it was far too early in the day for that.

Okay, not good.

I sighed, "What is it? Don't tell me another anonymous phone threat."

"Lys, I need you to sit down. Is Johns with you?" he asked.

"I mean, he's here...but it is his house. I just walked in the office. Why?" Now I was worried and worried meant pacing the floor. I hated bad news calls and having a large enough space to release the tension was to my liking.

I heard Jake draw a deep breath. "Have you or he seen the latest issue of Rocktower?"

His words came carefully as he referred to the regional daily magazine that circulated in mostly fan groups. It was nearly the equivalent of purchasing and reading the National Enquirer if it was all about rock and metal music.

As if he could see me, I shook my head, "No. I mean I haven't."

"Listen, I need you to be calm," his tone becoming more measured by the second. It was if he knew I would blow and truth be told, if he was already instructing me to keep my cool, I was definitely going to do just that.

Shaking my head, I wedged the phone between my neck and ear, and marched to the kitchen. Tossing the phone, I hit the speaker button before snatching the pile from in front of Ioan. I flipped through the thick stack. "No, but I've got them right here—"

My heart fluttered, the blood running like slow ice water in my veins. I wasn't sure whether to be pissed off or frightened.

"Lys? You with me?" Jake's voice a calm beacon in my storm of rage. "I need you to breathe."

My words shook, "What the fuck, Jake?"

"Lys." He ordered, "Lys...I need you to breathe."

I couldn't believe my eyes. It was a violation that I wasn't able to put into words. While a bit blurry in certain respectful places, the image of Ioan and I engaged in a sex act last night was remarkably clear. I sat atop him, on the laundry room floor, my head thrown back while one of his hands was trained on my clit and the other pinched a nipple. I guess I was lucky those were where the blurring effect had been used.

I wanted to vomit.

Ioan pulled the phone to his face. "What the fuck is this, Merritt?" he snarled. "Who took that fucking picture?"

"Ioan I know you're upset and I understand why. It's a complete violation of privacy—"

"You're goddamn right it is! I don't let the press into my space. Ever," his face filled with rage.

Jake remained calm, "I'm guessing this wasn't another pretend show. How long?"

"Jesus Christ," Ioan bit in retort. "No, it wasn't, clearly."

"How long?" he asked again.

"Why the fuck does that matter?" Ioan growled.

I took a breath to center myself. Jake was trying to find out how long our real relationship had been happening so he could put it in the timeline of events. Everything going on was a clue and could bring us closer to the stalker. The attacks on Ioan were ramping up, but for what purpose? Were they trying to get Ioan to break up with me or rather Lyssie? The dead animals and notes were one thing, but a rattlesnake in a box of flowers? Pictures from outside the record label and his backyard, nearly being shot, twice, and a gas leak at a cabin no one knew we were at and now this? Maybe the plan was to drive Ioan crazy instead.

I felt dizzy and the nausea consumed my insides. Sweat formed beads on my temples and I honestly thought I would topple over at any moment.

How long had it been since Ioan and I first had sex? The mere idea of anyone outside the two of us having that knowledge made the churning in my stomach worse. Had everyone been briefed? Had Fox looked at this picture? He would probably laugh and say something dickish. Closing my eyes, I inhaled deep, trying to breathe through the waves of sickness.

"Ioan, so far, I've got Bett running interference as she hacks her way through Rocktower's system. We are trying to seek out how they got the picture and destroy it as well. I need to know how long you have been sleeping together so I know how far back to look," he explained.

"Two weeks," I finally choked out, as I admitted to my best friend, but more importantly, my *boss* that I started fucking our client right under his nose.

The phone was silent for so long, I thought we lost the connection until I heard Jake take a deep breath again. "Lys...I'm sorry. I'll make sure Bett gets this cleared up as fast as possible. Call me later, okay?"

Tears stung my eyes as I forced an "Okay" before disconnecting the call. I wasn't sure if I should cry or scream or do both. So, I stood with my hands flat against the cold of the marble bar trying to not hyperventilate. I was angry, sure, but I was also a little scared now. A stranger injected themselves into something so personal and it made my skin crawl. I felt dirty.

The heat of Ioan's eyes were on me just before his thick arms pulled me into his chest. I went limp like the very act of standing couldn't be done because I had no skeleton. Lifting me into the air, Ioan wrapped my legs around his waist and carried me down to the music room.

The darkened room containing a variety of instruments was noticeably cooler than the rest of the house. I kept my eyes closed and my head buried in Ioan's neck as I felt him kicking the piano bench out and away to make room for us. He sat, careful to miss the edge of the keys as he did. I breathed in the fresh scent of his soap, a smell I had recently attached to comfort and something else I had a difficult time naming.

His hands left my back, but I remained attached to him like some frightened animal hugging a tree trunk. His fingers pressed on the keys gently and the action hammered softly on the strings, creating a haunting sound in the deafening silence of the room. Under my hip, I felt his leg rise and fall on a petal to dampen the sound. Ioan's lips hovered near my ear and his voice was deep and husky; like fine whiskey and sweet smoke.

"Drawn down I find my facade stripped away...my shadow gives way to light. I've fallen away, taken away...this sweet insanity..." Ioan crooned his slow, melodic and lilting tune. "I lay my sword at your feet...this demon's heart is yours by right...overtaken by your light. This sweet insanity...my possession is complete."

By the time he finished the song, rivers of tears fell from my eyes, soaking his shirt. Scooping my face in his hands, he thumbed the streams away and searched my eyes. "Alyssa, I am so sorry. I never meant to hurt you."

"What?" My eyes refocused on his.

"This is my fault. I never thought about how exposed we were last night. I won't make that mistake again," Ioan brushed the last of my tears from my cheeks then gave me a soft kiss. "I promised you safety here and I failed."

My throat was dry and I struggled to swallow the lump growing inside. I didn't blame him for that picture; I blamed the asshole that took that picture. How dare they encroach on his sanctuary; it was a violation on both of us.

"Why did you bring me down here?" I whispered. His deep chocolate eyes roamed over me like they were inspecting me for any sign of damage.

"No windows. No outside access," his fingers gently sweeping a lock of hair behind my ear. "Just me renewing a promise to you."

Chapter Thirty-Seven

Ioan

We stayed in the music room for several hours disconnected from the outside world. While I knew I couldn't make everything right, I could, at least momentarily, distract her from what happened. She didn't want me to blame myself, but I did.

It was nearly six when we emerged from the downstairs, ending up back in the kitchen searching for food. Alyssa's phone, still lying on the bar, flashed frantically with a substantial amount of missed calls. I picked up the device and handed it to her as she walked by.

Shaking her head, she dropped it back on the counter, "They know where I am...if it were really important, Chico or Fox would have already charged inside."

"What about Daisy?" I replied.

Alyssa stopped in her tracks, spun on her heel before grabbing her phone again. I watched her flip through messages and one in particular made her smile. It was her real smile and that could only mean a text from Daisy.

Her forested eyes glinted with sheer joy, "I need to call home."

"Of course!" I grinned. "I'll order dinner."

Before I could turn to give her any sort of privacy, I heard the ringing through the speakerphone and a "Hey sweetheart!" when the call was answered. I walked toward the office, taking the opportunity to order Chinese delivery and answer an email from Mikal.

His email requested an update on when I would get my portion of the contract signed. My immediate thought was to respond with *'When I damn well please'* but I thought better of it.

> Mikal, Once the attorney is finished looking over the contract and gives his okay, I'll have it to you. Maybe tomorrow. —Ioan

That was the best I could do under the circumstances. Alyssa hadn't heard from Bett, so I would need to stall a little longer. I didn't want to explain why I hired a private security firm or the reason why they were reviewing my contract. I rounded back into the living room in time to catch the end of Alyssa's very in-depth conversation with her daughter.

"Are you sue-er, Mommy? I still don't fink they all have wings," Daisy said with quick confidence.

Alyssa smiled into the phone, "I have it on good authority they do...if they don't, then they're pixies, not fairies."

"Who toad you that?" The little girl clearly wasn't convinced.

"Oh, well, my friend Ioan knows all about those sorts of things. He's very smart," Alyssa offered.

"Okay, Mommy...if you're sue-er. I be-weave you," Daisy sighed, finally accepting her mother's explanation. My insides went soft at the sound of her sweet voice.

"Sweetheart, you let Kate read you a book and you go to bed...Mommy loves you and will see you very soon."

After a few more minutes, Alyssa released the call and sauntered back to where I stood at the threshold of the office, stopping short when she finally noticed me. Her smile a beacon that I was born to answer.

"Why don't you go up and get a shower and I'll meet you upstairs with dinner?" I wrapped my hands around her waist, pulling her into me. "We can lie in bed and ignore everything else outside these walls."

Her face wrinkled with uncertainty, "I'm not sure that's a good idea, Ioan."

"Why? Because of some dickhead that doesn't understand boundaries? Alyssa, look around you," I made a motion with my hand to the windows. "I've already shut this house down. And tomorrow, I'm calling that contractor back and having them install blinds in the mudroom."

She still looked dubious.

"If this is about Jake or anyone else knowing, that's fine. I mean, the timing is a little off, but they were going to know anyway, right?" An arrogant grin pulled at my mouth, "Not sure if you've noticed, but I'm kind of obsessed with you."

My comment finally elicited an eyeroll and a giggle.

"It does sound nice," she admitted coyly. "You've got a deal."

Twenty minutes later, I paid the driver for our food and climbed the stairs to my bedroom. The shower was still running as steam billowed around the barely open door of the ensuite bathroom. I had to fight the urge to strip down and join her because knowing she was just feet from me, wet and naked, made me near feral.

Cursing my resistance under my breath, I sat the bag of food containers on the side table and plopped on the bed to wait. Alyssa's phone lay near her pillow, buzzing wildly. Concerned she was missing something important, I picked it up to take it to her in the bathroom. It vibrated again in my hand as a new text flashed across her screen.

Am I usually a nosy person who reads over someone's shoulder? No, absolutely not. But I couldn't help but notice the three missed calls and ceaseless messages coming through all at once. The small avatar looked like a pink haired anime character and had the name Tech Goddess attached. There was no doubt it was Bett.

As I took a stride to the bathroom door the phone vibrated again, but this time I saw the full message as large as life.

> Lys! Seriously…The call is coming from inside the house. It's in the contract…The record company has rights to everything if something…

Rights? What does she mean rights? Then another message.

> Big Handsome is in serious trouble. Call me! I know you're inside. Stavopolos is real bad news. He's behind…

"What the hell?" I muttered. The messages were cut off and since I couldn't get into her phone, it was all I had. Could Mikal really be involved? It was almost absurd to think about. Mikal couldn't possibly stoop to such a level as to send dead animals via messenger service or hire someone to shoot up my house. Why would he do that? There had to be a mistake. Did he really want me dead? Throwing the phone back on the bed, I considered only one option for all of twelve seconds.

Grabbing my keys off the large dresser, I bounded down the stairs nearly sprinting for the garage. I would get answers for everything that happened, but more importantly, if he was involved, I would get revenge for everything that happened to Alyssa.

Chapter Thirty-Eight

Alyssa

I stood under the hot stream of water until my scalp was raw and the pounding of the shower head no longer vibrated in my teeth. It felt so good to wash the day off and I considered staying right where I was until the spray drilled a hole through me. But, Ioan was waiting and other than Daisy, he was the only person I would leave this solace for. The air was cool as I stepped out of the glass door of the shower and through the bathroom threshold, wrapping my long hair up.

"Ioan?" I called out, pulling a second towel around me and securing it with a little tuck near my armpit. I smelled garlic and ginger and I turned in the direction of the scent. Sitting on the bedside table was a large plastic bag containing several paper boxes, the aroma coming from them made my mouth water.

Walking to the bedroom door, I leaned out, calling to the house, "Hey, Ioan!"

No answer.

Jesus...where did he go?

I turned back to find my phone still on the bed, but flashing erratically. "Aww, crap."

I punched in my four digit code, Daisy's birthday, and scrolled through seven missed calls; two from Jake, five from Bett. My heart

raced because I couldn't believe what could be so important that Bett
would have called me so many times. Skipping over the call list, I
clicked on the text icon.

> Lys, pick up our phone. I need to talk to you.

> Girl, what are you doing? This is muy impor-
> tante.

> Lys, if your phone is on silent and I have to
> hack it, I swear I'll make your ring tone the
> Oompa Loompa song forever.

"Shit." I growled.

> Lys! Seriously…The call is coming from in-
> side the house. It's in the contract…The
> record company has rights to everything if
> something happens to Ioan, all his money
> goes to Siren Records. Girl! Call me.

> Big Handsome is in serious trouble. Call
> me! I know you're inside. Stavopolos is real
> bad news. He's behind everything all the
> way back to the initial stalking. Long story,
> but I've checked bank records, travel docu-
> ments, the gamut. It's him, I'm sure of it.

I felt my face flush, "Shit, shit, shit!"

I dialed Bett and she picked up immediately, "Lys!"

"Give me the down and dirty…quickly," I ran down the hallway
to my bedroom, which was really just a glorified closet at this point.
Putting Bett on speaker, I grabbed whatever clothes were in my quick
reach and started dressing.

"FYI, Jake is here. Now for the deets," I heard her clacking away on
her keyboard. "I checked the contract like you asked using a program

that filtered out all the legal gobbledygook so I could get a better idea of what the meat and potatoes were."

I sighed, "Faster Bett, please."

"Yeah, okay," she typed faster. "Upon the read over it seems as though Siren Records and Mikal Stavopolos are the sole heirs of Big Handsome's estate should he come to his demise. Just to be sure, I hacked into the label's legal archives and he's been signing some version of this for years. But just him, not the other members. Also, there is a huge life insurance policy on him with Stavopolos as the sole beneficiary."

"Keep going," I shoved my feet into my combat boots and tied them in record time. Picking up my phone, I ran down the stairs looking for Ioan, but something in my gut felt off. Finding my purse, I pulled my gun out and checked the clip.

"None of the other band members have the same contract, just Big Handsome. Like I said, I checked his bank records and with my mad skills, found several large cash withdrawals that look like they could be payments," Bett hurried to get to her point.

"Payments for what?" I started clearing the house, room by room.

"Lys, these look like payments for services rendered," Jake explained. "And by the looks of it, these are to some folks I wouldn't trust to pick up my trash. Lys, Stavopolos is the only one with the means and motive to pull this off...and worse yet, Fox reported the manager, Marco, has been acting out of character."

I froze. I was right.

"Out of character, how?" I rounded the corner to the gym but found it empty.

"He's a gambler, Lys...usually Blackjack. But five days ago, he quit cold turkey. I had Bett check his phone records. Turns out he's had a side piece in New Jersey for decades. All of a sudden, no more calls or money transfers to his girl."

My mind raced with the implications. If the stalking was fabricated by Mikal to intimidate Ioan into staying with Siren Records, then he obviously thought Ioan had more control over the band than he did. I knew Bett already vetted the band prior to our taking the case. Obliterate's value, cumulatively, teetered around one-hundred million dollars. Mikal couldn't afford to lose that kind of money and who better than Ioan to place his bets on. He knew Ioan had no family left after the death of his mother earlier this year and with no serious relationship on the horizon, paying someone, or several someone's, to do a little light stalking was money well spent if it kept Ioan in line and where he was.

He didn't bank on Ioan taking matters into his own hands and hiring Onyx.

Me entering the picture as Ioan's new "girlfriend" must have sent Mikal into a tailspin. If Ioan fell in love with Lyssie Blackwell, she might support him in a decision to change labels or convince him to settle down and tour less. Either way, Lyssie Blackwell or Ioan Johns had to go, and with a large life insurance policy in place, the answer was clear.

"He's blackmailing the manager," my breath shortened as I jogged around the last corner of the house.

"That's our thinking as well," Jake replied. "Lys, what are you do-ing?"

"Looking for Ioan," I snapped. "Shit."

"What's wrong, my princess?" Bett sounded concerned. She had a way of nicknaming people during times of stress. Apparently, today I was Princess.

I huffed, "Ioan's gone."

"Not to worry!" I heard Bett's fingers clacking over the keys, "I'll find Big Handsome—"

"No need, Bett," I said flatly, picking up a small, rectangle plastic box from the driveway. "He's pulled the tracker from his car. As if that would stop me. Jake?"

"Yeah, Lys, I'm here," he affirmed.

"Get Fox and Chico to Stavopolos' house. I've got the office."

Chapter Thirty-Nine

Ioan

I wish I could have said my Mercedes squealed to a stop when I slammed on the brakes near the rear door of the Siren office tower. That would have been satisfying as hell. I was surprised, however, to find the rear door unlocked on a Sunday. I started to march past the empty security desk, when an older man in a dark blue uniform stopped me as he exited the nearby restroom.

"Sir! You'll need to sign in," he called after me as I approached the elevator.

There was no way I was letting anyone get in my way.

"Sorry, I just forgot something upstairs. I'll be right down." I replied as the doors slid open.

The security guard's face reddened, "Listen here, it's my job if you don't sign in and let me know where you're headed. I ain't losing my job for you."

"I'll be right down," I jabbed the floor number and the doors slid shut again. I wasn't trying to sneak in to confront Mikal, but I didn't want someone tipping him off either. Still trying to piece it all together, my mind was racing as fast as my heart. I couldn't believe that he would pull something like this and that little internal voice screamed for a reason.

I was almost disappointed that I couldn't get into Alyssa's phone. I wanted so many more details than I had before bursting through his door. Was this all just a media scheme? Something to boost album sales? Even with our worst performing album, we still hit multi-platinum status. There would be no need for Mikal to fake a stalker for a sales boost.

None of it was making sense.

The only other thing I felt, besides confusion, was some deep anger that filled my veins and came from some other place. No matter why Mikal had done all of this, he put Alyssa in real danger. I was fully aware of how ridiculous it all sounded since her job was quite literally, being in danger most of the time. But, this was different. While I'd like to think Obliterate's fans were all good people of sound mind, I was a realist and I knew that wasn't always the case. Fan's going crazy over a perceived threat happened all the time. We'd seen it time and again with other bands that were friends of ours. All that needed to happen was one person to take anything Mikal put in the rumor mill seriously and she could end up hurt, or worse.

And I wasn't forgetting about the picture from last night.

The elevator's chime dinged and the doors opened right into the Siren Records reception area. It was a Sunday, so the lights were mostly off and the entire entry was deserted. I strode to the door of his office and banged on it with the side of my closed fist. "Mikal? You in there?"

I tried the handle, but it was locked.

"Mikal? Seriously...open the door, I saw your ugly ass car outside," my fist slammed on the door again.

Leaning in, I listened for any sound on the other side and to my surprise, I heard two very low, very muffled voices. I knocked once more, "Mikal!"

I moved away just as the heavy entrance flew open and he stood in the threshold, "I beg your pardon, Ioan. Stacey and I were...working on some numbers."

Looking behind his shoulder I found his young secretary straightening her shirt and wiping her mouth. This man was truly disgusting. Mikal stepped aside, allowing me to pass as the woman gathered her purse and slipped her shoes onto her feet. She glared at me as she drew close.

"I'll see you tomorrow, sir," she smiled at him as she threaded the needle between us.

Mikal shut the door.

He stared at me for a long moment before clasping his hands together. "So, Ioan, what can I do for you this evening? I assume this is about your contract. I read your email earlier. Although..." he paused, his back to me as he stared out of the window. "I really wished you would have let the corporate lawyers take a look for you. I mean, at least they know what they're doing."

"The assumption being that any lawyer I hire wouldn't know what to look for?" I asked.

Mikal whirled on me with a look of anger, but he kept his voice weirdly calm, "I'm not sure what you mean. Except that we have the best legal team in the industry...I'm not sure you could find anyone better."

"Why would it matter if I hired my own attorney? I mean, you aren't hiding anything in there, right?" I gave him an innocent chuckle and prayed he would take the bait.

"Why would you ask that?" Fury and something akin to fear flashed in his eyes. It seemed like I touched a nerve and that was all I needed to confirm what Bett sent to Alyssa.

"I don't know, Mikal. Why does Siren get everything if something happens to me?" I crossed my arms over my chest and felt a twinge of satisfaction when he flinched at the question.

"I don't know what you're talking about, Ioan," he waved his hand at me. "I think you're spending too much time with that little groupie."

His casual dismissiveness and his disrespect of Alyssa was starting to piss me off. My hands dropped to my sides, clenching into fists. He probably thought I knew everything, but I didn't; so instead of just beating his ass now, I decided to go fishing.

"I think you do know, Mikal. I think you've been banking on me being completely blind to everything...but that's over. I know. I know what you've been up to," as the words spilled from my mouth, scenes from the past several months and weeks flashed in my head as if my subconscious was doing the guess work for me.

He raised a thick brow, "Oh? And what is that?"

"Quit the bullshit, you're behind the stalking and everything else these past few months," I growled.

Mikal offered me a cold laugh, "Oh, am I? Who told you that? The little groupie? Boy, I can't believe you'd let a little cunt like that get in your head."

That was all I needed, I rushed forward, driving my fist into his nose. I felt the sickening crack under my knuckles as his nose broke and blood sprayed across the carpet. Mikal doubled over, bellowing in pain.

"You call Alyssa one more name, and I'll give you a jaw to match that nose!" I yelled. "You're son of a bitch, you know that? Why, Mikal?"

He stood, wiping the blood along the arm of his shirt. "You ungrateful son of a bitch! I have done everything for you...everything! You would be nothing without me. So what if I sent you a few letters or leaked a few pictures...you were getting out of line! I know you've been talking to other labels...I hear things, Ioan. I know things."

I was getting out of line? Like he's my pimp and this was his way of keeping me, keeping Obliterate in our place? But before I could formulate my next response, he opened the top drawer of the large mahogany desk and pulled out a gun.

"Mikal. What are you doing?" I demanded. Now everything seemed so surreal and I had to convince myself that Mikal Stavopolos, the owner of my record label, was holding a gun on me.

ME.

He pursed his lips, swiping at his nose again, "You know, Ioan. All you had to do was play along. Keep being the lonely, sad, misunderstood talent so we could keep making money. But, no! You just couldn't stay in your place."

"Mikal, put the gun away," I raised my hands in front of me. "You don't want to do this."

That's what I was supposed to say, right?

His laugh was downright frozen, "Oh, but I do. You see...you're still under a contract with Siren and by extension, me. So, when you have your little accident today—" His voice trailed off and he shrugged, "Well, let's just say, I will mourn your death as a very wealthy man."

I shook with anger, "You know what? Fuck off Mikal. Do it...kill me. I'll die knowing that you won't see a dime of whatever you think you're going to get. Alyssa will make sure of that."

"You think *she's* going to stop me? Ioan, you've signed over your entire life to me. Everything you have...your music, your house, and that American-made piece of shit you're so fond of driving is mine. You know? Come to think of it...maybe I'll take that piece of ass you've got too...she's got a nice set of tits," his smirk made even more ominous as the blood dried around his mouth. "I like a bitch with some tits."

"If you touch even one strand of hair on her head, I will end you," I snarled, grinding my teeth. I felt the heat rising in my chest as the thought of Mikal putting his hands on her drove me to near madness. I inched forward to loom over him. He may have had a gun, but I was much bigger and for sure faster.

I wouldn't have the chance to find out, because as I took my next step, Alyssa burst through the door of the office.

Chapter Forty

Alyssa

Thankfully, I was observant, otherwise, I'd never be able to find the keys to the car in the first place and there was zero chance in me waiting for an Uber. If I hadn't been in agent mode, I would have really enjoyed driving the Hellcat. Peeling around the corner of the thirty-eight-story edifice, I hit the brakes on the car, screeching to a stop next to Ioan's Mercedes. He was already here.

Hitting Fox's face on my phone, it only rang once before he picked up, "Yeah."

"He's here." I slammed the door on the car before jogging to the entrance.

"Is the target with him?" Fox barked.

Turning, I scanned the parking lot, "Affirmative. I have eyes on the target's vehicle. I'm going inside."

Before Fox could offer any argument or demand that I wait for back up, I yanked on the doors and strode inside. An older man of about seventy stood as I entered, but I barely noticed as my eyes fixed on the elevators.

"Now, Miss...you're going to have to sign in. I can't be letting anyone else just go upstairs without checking in," he demanded gently.

I picked up the clip board and scribbled my name before turning back to the bank of elevators.

"Hold on...which office you heading to? I'll need to call up and announce you," he said.

"No!" I snapped. "Don't do that. Call the police. There's a dangerous man on the top floor and I'll need back up."

The old man's eyes widened, but he jumped to attention, "Yes ma'am!"

Running for the elevator, my fist slammed on the call button. I entered the car, but before the doors slid shut, I watched the old security guard speak into the receiver of his phone. The doors slid shut and as the elevator rose, I checked my phone to make sure I was recording and the tiny wireless mic that I placed in my left ear was connected to the app. The elevator's chime rang and I stepped out. My boots sank into the plush carpeting and made no noise as I crossed the reception area to the door leading to Mikal's office.

I heard angry voices just beyond the barrier so I leaned in, my right ear just barely touching the wood.

"You know what? Fuck off Mikal. Do it...kill me. I'll die knowing that you won't see a dime of whatever you think you're going to get. Alyssa will make sure of that." I heard Ioan bark.

My blood started to boil. From the sound of the conversation, Mikal most likely had a weapon on Ioan, which pissed me off. But also, why the hell was Ioan goading him? Mikal was desperate now, like a wild animal that's been cornered and I was sure he'd lash out.

"You think *she's* going to stop me? Ioan, you've signed over your entire estate to me. Everything you have...your music, your house, and that American-made piece of shit you're so fond of driving is mine. You know? Come to think of it...maybe I'll take that piece of ass you've got too. She's got a nice set of tits."

He paused, then, "I like a bitch with some tits."

"If you touch even one strand of hair on her head, I will end you." Even I heard the growl emanate from somewhere deep inside Ioan. If Mikal was the deer, then Ioan was the lion. I had to get inside and put a stop to this before he did something and got hurt.

I slowly clasped my left hand around the handle, careful not to make a sound until I was ready. Pulling my gun from my back waistband, I flipped the safety off. Turning the handle, I felt the latch release and wasted no time throwing the door wide. Immediately, I had Mikal in my sight.

His arms shifted, and he pointed his small hand gun at me.

"Put the gun down, Stavopolos," I ordered, my eyes fixed on his.

"Jesus, Ioan, can't you go anywhere without her?" his eyes rolled in disgust.

From this point, I knew I had not just the LAPD on route, but Fox and Chico as well. But it was a game of who would arrive first. If the police did, I could talk my way into speaking with the officer-in-charge and after that, it wouldn't take three minutes for me to legitimize my presence. I knew how to play the game, but I didn't want to. I needed my team to be first on scene.

Regardless of who showed up when, I had to get a confession. That was the only way to seal the coffin on Mikal. He would have to admit he was behind it all: stalking, the leaked photos, and the attempted murder.

"Tell me, Mikal...why'd you do it?" I kept my gun and my voice steady. I wanted answers, I didn't want to provoke him. Out of my periphery, I watched Ioan edge his way toward me.

Mikal let out a piercing laugh, "As I was just telling your boyfriend, if he could have just played along...let the press in on his little stalker, everything would have been fine. But then *you* happened."

"It's more than that, isn't it Mikal? You could have leaked the stalker story to the press yourself...but you didn't. I mean, you were behind it anyway. Why not go all the way and just tell them?" I had to keep him talking. The longer we stood here, the better our chances.

"Ha!" He coughed out a choked laugh. I imagined whatever Ioan did to his face was allowing blood to run down his throat. "You don't know, do you sweetheart? That's a shame. You see, your boyfriend doesn't like the press. He doesn't like them knowing too much about him. I wasn't even supposed to know about the stalker. He needed a viral moment...but instead—"

He shrugged.

I shook my head, "No, Mikal. This isn't about press. This is about you keeping Ioan and by extension, the band under your control. You couldn't stand the thought that maybe the guys might see the greener grass, could you? So, instead of sweetening the deal with Siren Records, you decided to scare Ioan into staying. The dead rat was a message, right? Ioan took it as a crazed fan, but you meant it as a threat. Isn't that right?"

His head tilted at an odd angle, as if a thought just occurred to him. He stood quiet for what felt like too many moments to count before his eyes narrowed on me, "Who the fuck are you, sugar tits?"

The growl from Ioan emerged like something buried in the earth. It rumbled and I thought I felt it in the air.

"Ah, ah, ah," Mikal tsked, shaking the barrel of the gun at Ioan. His eyes immediately darted back to mine. "I asked you a question. Who the fuck are you, Lyssie Blackwell?"

I ignored his question, "When I came into the picture, you freaked out. One minute, Ioan is an orphan in the world, the next he has someone to care about...maybe even love. You decided to go full tilt...if he was just screwing some groupie, that was one thing, but a live-in girlfriend was another ballgame. You needed Ioan dead so you could cash in on the life insurance policy."

Ioan was so close to me, his sweat mixed with his cologne creating an otherwise titillating scent. Not an appropriate thought at the time, but if I didn't have a gun in my face and we weren't in the gaudiest office known to man, we'd have a repeat of last night. My dirty thought disappeared as his head whipped around to me then back to Mikal.

"What life insurance? Alyssa, what are you talking about?" he ordered.

I tipped the barrel of my gun at Mikal, "Why don't you ask him?" I paused as my target narrowed his eyes on me, "Go ahead, tell him."

If his eyes were razors, I would have already bled out. I watched the corner of his eye twitch and he licked his lips. He knew his game was over but to my surprise, he composed himself, drawing a deep breath. The shift was sudden and I didn't know if he was just scared of being found out or truly a sociopath. "I asked you a question...who are you Lyssie Blackwell?"

"Mikal!" Ioan snapped and Mikal's eyes met his. "You really are a piece of shit. You would have done it, wouldn't you? Kill me."

"You should have stayed in your place! Your only job was doing what I told you and be content with your pathetic life," Mikal pointed the gun at Ioan's chest as his hand and arm began to shake. This wasn't good. He was starting to spiral out of control and was in fact capable of anything at this point.

Where the hell was my team?

Mikal continued, "You were going to take the band away from me...and I couldn't let you do that." His head bobbed, "But, I think I know how to teach you the lesson you need to learn. I've been thinking about it for a while. It's her. She has to go."

His arm snapped back to me and before I even heard the gun fire, Ioan shoved me into an armchair and stepped into my place. Without a second thought, I fired, hitting Mikal in the shoulder, and watched as he buckled to the ground dropping his gun. I whipped my head to where Ioan stood, his hand covering his chest.

He was hit.

"Ioan!" I screamed, as to my horror, his knees gave away under him and he too, fell to the floor.

Rage like I had not felt since I was a teenager exploded from me as I ran to Mikal, kicking his gun away. I stomped the heel of my thick tactical boot into his injured shoulder and he shrieked wildly. I leaned down as he writhed under me, "You want to know who I am? I'm the bitch that will hunt you down and destroy you if Ioan dies."

I removed my foot from his shoulder and kicked him in the balls.

Turning around, I pulled a very expensive looking table runner from the cocktail bar and ran back to Ioan, dropping to my knees, "Hey...Ioan, you need to open your eyes. I need you to look at me."

I wadded the cloth and pressed hard into his chest as my eyes tried to avoid the pool beginning to soak into the carpet next to him. "Ioan! Goddamn it! Ioan!"

"I'm here, baby...I'm here," his eyes fluttered. "Does it make me a wimp if I say it hurts?"

"No," tears welled in my eyes and I choked a small chuckle. "Just...stay with me Ioan, okay. Promise me."

His head bobbed once before the room exploded with Fox and Chico and a rush of police close behind. I kept pressure on Ioan's wound as my partner tried to get a handle on the situation. Everything around me moved like slow motion. All movement deliberate and orchestrated and every sound dampened. Chico pulled me back to allow the paramedics to work on Ioan, but once he did, I felt like stone; cold and motionless. It was only when they had him loaded onto a gurney and heading for the door did I pull out of my stupor.

"I'm going with him!" I yelled, sprinting after them and sliding in just as the elevator door shut.

Chapter Forty-One

Alyssa

"Ioan! Ioan! Don't you die on me!" I screamed in Ioan's face as I ran beside the paramedics as we entered the large bay.

"Ma'am...I need you to stay here!" The tall blonde man ordered as his partner pulled the gurney through heavy steel doors.

Tears fell like rivers from my eyes and I watched through the small window as they wheeled him around a corner and out of sight. I touched the glass. It was cold against my finger tips. I wanted more than anything to barge through those doors if only to make sure everyone did their job and he survived.

What if he didn't?

The thought made my stomach churn and I almost expelled everything inside me right in the hallway. A mix of adrenaline and fear writhed in my body. I kept my eyes targeted on any movement beyond the doors but guessed all the action took place well beyond my sight.

"I love you," my words fell like morning dew off velvety leaves.

What was I supposed to do now?

Taking a deep breath, reality began to seep in; Mikal. The simple mention of his name made my blood boil. Mikal had been behind this the entire time. With Ioan dead, he would have full control over all of Obliterate's music including any royalties that Ioan would have earned. As more adrenaline flowed freely through my veins, the picture was all too clear.

Because Ioan wasn't alone anymore or under Mikal's perceived control, he was worth more dead than alive. And now, Mikal still may actually get it all. That piece of shit orchestrated everything.

Damn it, Ioan. That bullet was meant for me. Mikal was aiming for me.

More tears fell as I circled the waiting room trying to figure out what to do. I knew I should call someone, but who? Not Marco. Although Mikal never admitted it, I was sure he blackmailed Marco into his participation, whatever it was. I needed Jake but that call was for me, not Ioan. Ioan needed someone too.

Was I his person?

Pulling out my cell phone, I dialed the only other family I could think of; only three words and he didn't hesitate.

"I'm on my way." And thirty minutes later, Ezra ran through the automated doors of the Cedars-Sinai Emergency department.

"Lyssie?" breathless, his face twisted with pain. "Where is Ioan? How is he?"

I shook my head, "Surgery. I haven't heard anything."

"What the hell happened?" his eyes roamed over me.

"We found the stalker," my voice cracking as I struggled to stay calm. I didn't know if I could do this. I wasn't good at the bad news, and this being the man I loved made it so much worse.

"Who?!"

"Mikal Stavopolos," I whispered hoarsely but continued before he could interrupt. "He was only trying to scare Ioan into staying at the label...but when I suddenly arrived, he realized it was more than a possibility that he and the band might actually consider another offer. He would lose everything...especially with what was written into Ioan's contract."

Ezra's face contorted in confusion, "What are you talking about? What was in Ioan's contract?"

"Mikal was the sole beneficiary of Ioan's estate if he died...including rights to Obliterate's music," I replied. I watched the understanding wash over him as the outrage flooded his face.

"How do you know that?" he eyed me carefully, his jaw tight. "Are you sure?"

My lips pursed, "Positive. Ezra, my team and I...we're a lot more than you realize."

"I know more than you think. Your name is Alyssa Salerno, you're from Seattle, and we hired Onyx Industries because it is a multi-million dollar security firm whose clients range from royalty to the state foster system," he said quietly, recognizing the shock on my face. "I want to know how you found out about Mikal."

I fought the urge to back the conversation up, "It was in the contract...without a will or dependents, Mikal wrote himself as beneficiary. All the clues added up. Only Mikal would have the knowledge of Obliterate's movements and the financial means to hire a hit man."

"That son of a bitch," he growled.

"There's more," I paused and led him to a corner of the waiting room where we could talk in private. I waited until we were seated before I continued. "Mikal also had a life insurance policy taken out on Ioan. Either way, Mikal would get his pay day."

"Where is Mikal?" the muscles in his chiseled jaw flexing tightly.

I shook my head, "I don't know. He was in pretty bad shape when I left his office with the paramedics."

Ezra eyed me and I realized he and Ioan had the same ability to ask a question without words. It was an annoying little habit, but I was too exhausted to fight it. "I'm pretty sure Ioan broke his nose...but I think the gunshot wound and the woman's size eight boot to the dick is what will put him in the prison infirmary for a few days."

"Yeah, I think that will do it," he chortled. Silence fell between us as our eyes locked and a mutual fear filled our space. The tears started to build again and I couldn't stop them. I also couldn't stand to cry in front of anyone let alone someone I barely knew. But before I could get control of my failing emotions, Ezra wrapped his large arms around my shoulders.

"He's going to be fine, Lys. No way in hell he's leaving you...or Daisy," he said softly.

I pulled away, "Daisy? He...told you about her?"

The kindest smile I had ever seen pulled at his lips, "He won't shut up about her...or you." He paused. "I've known Ioan most of my life...we know how to keep each other's secrets."

My heart skipped. I had no clue he had spoken about me, let alone my daughter, to anyone. Our worlds seemed fractured by what we showed the outside versus what we revealed to each other. Our own secluded safe space that others weren't allowed into. But knowing Ioan felt safe enough to let someone else into his heart felt...good because I was a part of it.

We sat in supportive silence for a long time as we existed together in our hope that Ioan would be alright. We were little more than strangers when I called him, but as the minutes ticked by, we were jumping over friendship and moving right into family. Those minutes turned into hours and by the second one, we were taking turns pacing the waiting room floor.

"This is worse than when we were kids," Ezra muttered under his breath, walking by me.

"You were with him...when the fire happened?" I whispered.

He nodded, "My mom and I waited in the hospital all night. She and Meredith were friends."

I wanted to know more about that night. I had so many questions that Ezra could shed a light on and more importantly, I wanted to know more about Meredith Johns. For a woman Ioan idolized, I knew she had to have been a phenomenal person.

"Lys!" Jake's voice called behind us. I turned to see my whole team, *my* family, in the threshold of the waiting room. Everyone, except Bett. Fox caught my eyes wandering and knew I was looking for her.

"She's taking care of something," his smile soft.

Jake wheeled his chair next to me as Ezra and I took seats facing him. His eyes searched mine looking for any news of Ioan's condition. I didn't need to say a word about my feelings or the past several weeks or explain that I had fallen for Ioan and that he felt the same; Jake knew and would have known even without the picture of us together.

"Come here, baby," he soothed, covering my entire body with his and I fell apart. Jake was the only person, other than Ioan, I felt completely safe with and knew any vulnerabilities wouldn't be judged or manipulated. The pressure from his hold stabilized my shuttering sobs, "Shhhh, he's going to be okay."

"You don't know that," my whisper muffled in his neck.

Shielding me from everyone, Jake's mouth leaned closer to my ear, "You're right. I don't...but I've got a feeling about it."

"That bullet was meant for me." I looked up from his chest to find his blue eyes staring down at mine.

"I know," he said quietly. "Which means he loves you enough to die for you. Don't waste that, Lys. When he wakes up, you jump in with both feet and don't live in the shadows anymore."

I didn't want to live like that. I wanted to be with Ioan for the rest of our lives if he wanted me. I never realized until I sat in that room, with two vastly different but simultaneously similar patchwork families next to me, that Ioan Johns broke bits of a stone heart away piece by piece.

Jake raised his brows telling me he meant what he said and I nodded. Before I could pull away, the sweetest sound in the world rang through the waiting room.

"Mommy!"

Leaning away, I looked at Jake in shock and he shrugged, "The family needed to be together."

"Mommy! Mommy!" Daisy called, jumping from Bett's arms with a small bag of M&M's. "Hi Mommy! Look what Aunt Bett got me!"

She wrapped her tiny arms around my neck, and I took in all of her. Her cheek against mine and her sweet kiss made me feel almost complete again. "Well, look at you, sweetheart, don't you look beautiful. Where did this dress come from?"

Holding her hand, she twirled on her tiptoes, and the blush colored fabric ballooned around her legs. My toddler looked at her auntie, and they both giggled; Bett's cheeks blushing the same color as her hot pink space buns.

"Oh, Auntie Bett got you another new dress, huh?" I laughed and she hopped back into my lap.

She popped a candy into her mouth, stared at Ezra, and chewed thoughtfully, "Mommy, who is that?"

"Daisy, meet Ezra. This is one of Ioan's very best friends," I smiled. "Do you remember me telling you about Ioan?"

She nodded.

Ezra held out his hand, "Very nice to meet you, Daisy."

To my utter surprise, Daisy immediately accepted the handshake, "Thank you. Do you want a MMM?"

"Sure, I'd love one," he smiled, plucking a green candy from her hand. "Thank *you*."

We waited in the room, all of us, for two more hours. The already waning daylight faded, and night reached out its hand to close us off from the reality outside. We watched entire families enter the waiting area and leave again, only to be replaced by another. Everyone took turns entertaining Daisy, who was being a very patient three-year-old.

At eleven o'clock, my phone vibrated with the hospital's number. Ezra and I went to the information desk where they told us to wait in a smaller, private room where the surgeon would meet us regarding Ioan. Daisy insisted on accompanying us to the desk, so I took her back, handing her to Bett. "Stay here with Bett and Fox and Chico, okay? Mommy will be right back." I paused, "Jake?"

Ten minutes later, as Ezra, Jake and I sat anxiously in a room no bigger than a cubicle, a middle aged man in blue scrubs and cap knocked then entered. "Ioan Johns' family?"

I froze. What was I supposed to say?

"Yes," Jake replied.

"First, Mr. Johns is resting in recovery. The small caliber bullet entered just above his third anterior rib, nicking the same rib on the posterior and lodging just against the scapula. We were able to remove the bullet and get the bleeding under control. He should make a full recovery," he explained.

Ezra let out a breath that told me he had been holding it since we walked in, "Thank God."

I felt the tears pool in my eyes, but I fought to pull them back, "I want to see him."

The surgeon nodded, "You can...as soon as he's moved to a room upstairs in the ICU. Depending on how he does there, he'll be moved to a private room in a few days."

Jake squeezed my hand before following the doctor and Ezra out of the room, but I stood locked in place. I was relieved he would be alright, but now I was also angry with him. Why did he step in front of me? I could have been the one in recovery right now and not him.

I thought of Daisy and again of Ioan and I understood.

It wasn't just me he was willing to die for but also for *her*. Ioan was willing to give his life for a tiny child he had never met. Daisy had already experienced more trauma in her short time on this planet than thousands of adults in their entire lives and leaving her without a mother wasn't something he was willing to risk.

I felt tears swelling again and this time I let them fall.

Chapter Forty-Two

Ioan

F lashes of Alyssa's screaming face ran through my head. I heard the loud crack of what sounded like a whip and searing pain. Her voice came again in a wave of sound until I realized I wasn't dreaming. I heard her voice; here, with me. I didn't have a clue how long I'd been out, but my body felt stiff and achy.

It was going to take several days of yoga to work out whatever this was.

Cracking an eyelid just to a slit, I blearily saw her sitting in a chair at the end of my bed. She held something yellow on her lap. Was that a doll? Maybe flowers? I concentrated on the voices. Voices, plural.

"...and they all lived happily ever after. The End." Alyssa said softly.

"I love that story," the small voice whispered. It was high pitched and more of a stage whisper than something intimate and quiet.

I knew it had to be Daisy.

"Mommy?"

"Yes, baby?" Alyssa replied quietly.

"When is daddy going to wake up?" Daisy sounded worried and that bothered me. No kid should have that level of concern, especially her.

"Oh, uhhm, Daisy," Alyssa stammered. "No baby...remember this is Ioan. Remember me telling you about Ioan?"

"Yeah...Daddy," Daisy strongly insisted.

"No, Daisy..."

The little girl continued unabated, "You said hims like me. See Mommy? Hims back is like my legs. That's Daddy."

She was a lot like her mother: opinionated and brilliant.

Alyssa stuttered, "Daisy, honey—"

I cleared my throat, rolling onto my back. "Alyssa," my voice like gravel. "She can call me whatever she wants."

"Ioan?!" She nearly whooped excitedly, "Oh my God...you're awake."

Opening my eyes, I saw the two most beautiful women on the planet staring back at me. One with the hazel-green eyes of a forest and the other with round pools of dark leather. I held my hand out to the tiny girl, "Hi Daisy...I'm so glad you came to see me."

Sitting her book on the end of my bed by my feet, she crawled into the bed, resting her body against my uninjured side. Alyssa tried to stop her, but I waved her off. Daisy picked up her book again and flipped the cover open.

"I'm going to tell you a story, okay?" she smiled. "Then, you need a nap."

I smiled down at the little girl nestled into the crook of my arm, "Anything you say."

When I looked back to Alyssa her face spoke volumes. I'm not sure if she wanted to laugh or cry, or maybe it was both. I knew she would be mad at me for stepping in the way of her shot, but I would be damned if I saw her in this bed, or worse.

"I'm going to go get the nurse," she smiled.

I nodded, "I'm in good hands here."

An hour after Daisy's story, it was her real nap time and luckily, Bett was more than happy to oblige. My parade of visitors was non-stop from there, so close to three o'clock, Alyssa finally closed the door so we could talk alone. I held my hand up for her to take it and when she did, I pulled her to the bed and I kept pulling on her until she was close enough for me to feel her lips on mine.

"I'm so glad you're alright," I said into her temple. But Alyssa pulled back and looked into my eyes, frowning.

"I wanted to be mad at you, after the surgeon said you would recover," she stated honestly. "For a split second I was."

I watched her face and etched every detail into my mind, "But?"

"But," she mumbled, picking little fuzzies off my blanket, "I understand why."

"Do you?" I laid my head back on the pillow to get a better look at her. "Really?"

Those woody eyes dug into my soul just like they did a month ago. It was a stare that blazed with fire and a fierce determination that I found just so damn hot. But, she was also trying to speak without words and again, I wasn't going to let her get away with it. "Out loud, Salerno. It's just us here."

She gave me an annoyed sigh and it made me chuckle.

"Yes, Johns...I do. Because I would have taken that bullet for you," she paused to touch my face. "And not because it was my job."

Taking her fingers I kissed them softly and held them against my lips, "I wasn't going to leave Daisy without her mom...and there was no way I wanted to live in a world without you."

We allowed our stares to linger on each other for a long moment. I wanted to take her all in, to sear her face in my memory like a brand. The pain of losing her would have been far worse than the throbbing in my chest and shoulder. And that was something I never wanted to think about again.

The corner of my mouth pulled into a sly smile, "You still mad at me?"

She tried so hard not to laugh and it was honestly the sexiest thing ever. "No. Only because you weren't a wimp about it."

My body wanted to double over in laughter, but the sharp pain radiating down my arm as I tried, brought me down to a well controlled chuckle and several groans. Alyssa's face turned to concern but I dismissed her worry. "I'm glad we could agree on that."

"I have an idea," she said, "New deal. You don't sign contracts with lunatics that want to kill you and I'll—"

"Alyssa," I rumbled, pulling her to my chest. "My turn for proposing deals."

She lifted a questioning brow at me.

"Get Jake to have your apartment packed and you and Daisy move to LA," I grinned, stroking her face with my fingers.

"I can probably do that. Might take a bit to find a place," she shrugged.

Wait. What did she say?

"Find a place? You have a place," I corrected.

She blinked, "Ioan...that's very kind. But—"

"No buts. Well, one but," I wrinkled my nose. "We won't be there long. It's not fit for a toddler...Daisy's going to need a yard and a play room. We *could* have a pool, but it'll need a fence until she learns to swim. We can find something for us...all of us. What do you say, Salerno?"

Epilogue

One year later...
  Present day

Chapter Forty-Three

Alyssa

I said yes. In every way.

I never left Ioan's side in the hospital. After surgery, he spent exactly twelve hours in ICU before he was moved to a private room where he finally woke around noon. Of course, he woke right in time to Daisy calling him her Dad. His answer? It was just fine by him, of course.

And he says I've got a hard head. Right.

Within three days, we were back home with Ioan sleeping in his own bed. I'm not exaggerating when I say it was a chore to keep him still and resting. He had so many plans about a new house and songs he needed to write running through his head that I finally gave up and Daisy and I camped in the theater most nights as he worked in the studio.

Daisy.

She was always a little shy around new people, always clinging to me for assurance. But with Ioan, their connection was immediate and undeniable, unconditional love. She looks at him with so much wonderment in her eyes, it captures your soul. Everywhere he goes, she is his shadow. And that captivation is mutual. He dotes on her like she is more precious than any jewel.

We were only home a few weeks when we received the call from the LA county prosecutor that Marco wouldn't be charged in connection to the stalking and attempted murder of Ioan. There were a lot of mixed emotions; I was furious, but he was quiet. On one hand, Ioan was torn up thinking that one of his closest allies betrayed him but on the other, he knew Marco felt trapped.

Mikal always had something on someone else. In Marco's case it was a gambling addiction and a long term affair with a hairdresser in New Jersey. In the end, Ioan was satisfied that the evidence wasn't there to tie the former band manager to everything and their contract together was over.

In early September, Ioan and the rest of Obliterate decided to put off the release of their new album until the following year. Weeks prior, the band was signed with an enormous label and new talent team and wanted the time to get acclimated to fresh ideas and people. And Ioan, still not fully recovered from his surgery, was grateful for the support and understanding of his bandmates and the new label. Nighttime Nic wasn't so happy to wait for new music, but, under the circumstances, he was gracious enough not to show his disappointment on air.

That same month, Ioan, Daisy, and I moved into our new home, officially relocating us to California. I thought my team would be sad or even angry that we wouldn't be within minutes of each other, but they weren't. Well, except for Bett. There were a lot of tears when we boarded the plane that last Sunday afternoon, until Jake reminded her Onyx had two private jets and we would only be an hour away.

Then, of course, there was Fox. A man who would like everyone to think that he was totally cool and that his partner of five years moving didn't bother him. Again, he's an asshole...and he's lying.

I've spoken to him every day.

I didn't work another case with my team until January. I felt like I needed time to adjust to my new life with my husband and our daughter. Oh, yeah, Ioan and I got married on Christmas Eve. It wasn't fancy. It wasn't Hollywood. But it was all family and love.

A year ago, if someone said that this is where I would be in my life, I would have laughed in their face. I had Daisy and Onyx and I was satisfied. But, I didn't have my other half. The lighter half. The part of my soul that pulled me from the darkness and forced me to live.

Not every woman needs a man. Or a woman. Or children. Or a dog. Or a cat. But, every person needs their person. That one soul that you feel connected to in the smallest and most intimate ways. Everyone needs their person and Ioan Johns is mine.

With the album release in May already hitting near double platinum status in its the first couple of months, the first leg of the US tour has been especially exciting for all the guys and the families. To celebrate the ninth album, *Revolutionary: Volume I*, they wanted to begin the tour in the city where it all started: San Diego.

Thirty minutes until show time, and I'm sitting in Ioan's dressing room waiting for him to leave the shower. When he finally emerges, he beckons me with a waggle of his finger to come toward him. But before I walk the few feet to him he freezes, looking around the room.

"Where's brown eyes?" he asks, referring to Daisy.

I smirk, "Kate took her to find dinner."

"Alright then," his cocky grin pulling wide as he scoops me into his arms. "Is that door locked?"

His skin is still slick and warm from his shower and I feel good wrapped in his embrace. I can still smell his soap; it's like cedar and salty air.

"Yeah, why?"

One brow raises, and he leans into my ear. His words send volcanic fire through me as he runs his warm hands under my shirt and around my waist, "Because, I'm going to make you scream my name, Alyssa."

I want this man so bad, but before I can protest with any reasonable argument about how quickly Kate could be back or that this wasn't exactly a very private room, he had me pinned to the wall, running his tongue along my neck.

"You know," he purred, "I've got a few hours, we could do this right."

"Ioan, you don't have a few hours. You have to get dressed...the show?"

He made a trail of kisses where his tongue just traced, "They can wait."

We both heard the soft knock at the door. I stared at him, then the door, and back at him, "I'll get it. You get dressed."

He turned back to the bathroom, groaning, emerging a few minutes later fully dressed and Daisy squealed when he appeared.

"Daddy!" she ran to him, leaping into his arms.

"Hey, Brown Eyes! How's my girl? Did Ms. Kate get you something to eat?" he smiled.

Daisy nodded, staring at his chest under his half-buttoned shirt. Her small finger traced over the letters of his most recent tattoo.

"D-A-I-S-Y" she recited aloud.

"That's right! And why is your name over Daddy's heart?" he asked.

She smiled, "Because I'm always in Daddy's heart."

"That's right, Brown eyes. Okay, Daddy has to work now, but, I'll see you in the morning, alright?" he kissed her cheek.

Kate took Daisy back to the hotel for the night while I walked with Ioan and the band to the side stage to watch the opening act. Five minutes before the set ended, I felt Ioan's arm wrap around my waist as he backed me into his hard chest.

"I've got to go get ready. I'll see you after...I hope you enjoy the show. I love you," he kissed the top of my head before buttoning his shirt up two more spaces. He's still a very private man.

I watch from the side as the mechanics of a concert are completed as one band comes off stage and the headliner goes on in the dark.

Programmed lights flash and the crowd whips into a frenzy. Then Ioan's silhouette appears back lit by a bright white light.

BOOM!

Simultaneously the stage goes pitch dark and giant pyrotechnics are shot in the air and he lets out a bone rattling roar.

Chapter Forty-Four

Ioan

I have never in my life felt more alive as I did when Daisy wrapped her arms around my neck for the first time and called me her dad. I love Ez's kids, my adopted nephews, and a new niece, Soren Elizabeth, but when Daisy is in the room, my world shines with a light that can't be described. There is nothing else for me but her and her mother.

My recovery was slow, but that's probably my own fault. I couldn't be sequestered to a bed when there was so much to do. When I purchased my home, I just wanted something normal and private but now there was so much more to consider. Where would Daisy attend school? What neighborhoods were private but not so much as to impede her having a normal childhood? I know I drove Alyssa crazy with all the considerations, but in the end, I think all the questions worked themselves out.

Then there was the music. From the moment I woke in the hospital, I felt inspired like I never had before. Lyrics and riffs swirled in my head and I had to get them out on paper. The downstairs studio became a beehive of activity from the second I could descend the stairs by myself. Alyssa and Daisy had quite a few sleepovers with Sean and Summit in the theater as the band worked at all hours. But, by the end, we had a completed album and more than enough for a second, with a little more work.

I thought very little about Mikal after that. I felt a little more disappointed in myself for trusting someone so completely to have my interests at heart. I knew better. I wasn't some wide-eyed kid off the street looking to get into the business. What I did was become complacent and that's what nearly ended my life. I would never allow it to happen again, because there was something so much bigger at risk: The life with my wife and daughter.

My proposal to Alyssa wasn't the most eloquent or even the most romantic. I did plan a better scenario, but when you have an almost four-year-old daughter who loves cotton candy and rides that spin, sometimes plans just become unhinged chaos. It was four days before Christmas, and I drove us all to the pier for a day of fun. I knew I wanted to do the whole down-on-one-knee thing, but I wasn't sure exactly when I would pull it off, but I did know we would be on the Ferris Wheel.

After a couple of hours of sweet treats and games, Daisy wanted to get on a couple of rides. Ride one went fine. Ride two? Well, let's say I ended up with bright pink vomit on my shirt and jeans. Poor kid.

Alyssa insisted we needed to leave, but Daisy, like her mother, had a determination made of titanium. She refused, saying only that if I carried her for a while, she would feel better. So I did and when we finally made it near that giant lighted wheel I had been waiting on all day, Alyssa reluctantly agreed to a ride. I waited until we were at the very top, our daughter sprawled sleeping over my shoulder, both of us covered in neon pink puke, to finally pull the ring box from my jacket.

Her eyes glistened with tears when I flipped the lid open with my thumb and she realized what was happening.

"I wanted this to be a little different today," I chuckled.

She looked from the ring then back to me, "Are you serious about this?"

"Baby, look at me. I smell like a carnival clown's wet dream. It doesn't get more serious than this." I paused as she laughed. "Alyssa, just say you'll marry me."

She said yes. And rewarded me later that night with a personal scrub down in the shower.

She said I took that vomit like a trooper.

We got married in our living room on Christmas Eve. It was a party we already planned with everyone we loved, so it just made sense to start our new lives, and the new year surrounded by them in the moment. We aren't flashy people anyway.

The band's new label has been nothing short of fantastic. While the story did hit a national audience, they were absolutely amazing about setting new dates for release and getting us back on tour. With everything that happened in the past several months, the guys and I decided to begin our fresh start, just like we did all those years ago, in San Diego.

In my dressing room, Alyssa sits cross-legged in a chair as I leave the bathroom after a quick shower. I curl my finger at her several times, enticing her to come to me. It never takes much for me to get turned on by her, and I am hard right now.

Shit.

"Where's brown eyes?" I ask.

Alyssa's pupils spread as they darted down to the towel wrapped at my waist, "Kate took her to find dinner."

I pull her into me and nod just beyond her, "Alright then. Is that door locked?"

"Yeah, why?" she leans into my neck and draws in a deep breath. Her exhale is warm on my skin as gooseflesh forms.

Running my hands under her shirt, I play with the band of her silk bra. "Because, I'm going to make you scream my name, Alyssa," my growl drips with lust as I pin her to the wall and slowly run my tongue along her neck.

"You know," I purr, "I've got a few hours, we could do this right."

"Ioan, you don't have a few hours. You have to get dressed...the show?" she responds with logic.

Why does she do that?

I trace a line of kisses down her neck, "They can wait."

A soft rap at the door and we both freeze. Alyssa's eyes dart from me to the door then back to me before she orders me to get dressed.

Party pooper.

But, I begrudgingly go back to the bathroom and dress. I walk out a few minutes later to words of welcome that steal my heart.

"Daddy!" Daisy calls out as she throws herself into my arms. I lift her high into the air as she squeals with delight.

"Hey Brown Eyes! How's my girl? Did Ms. Kate get you something to eat?" I ask, setting her on my chest.

She nods, and traces her finger over the letters of my new tattoo peaking from under my shirt.

"D-A-I-S-Y" she says.

"That's right! And why is your name over Daddy's heart?" I ask.

"Because I'm always in Daddy's heart."

"That's right, Brown eyes. Okay, Daddy has to work now, but, I'll see you in the morning, alright?" She nods and I give her a kiss before putting her on the floor.

Kate takes her by the hand, leading her through the winding hallways out of the stadium as Alyssa and I make our way to the stage to watch the opening band. They are phenomenal and as the large stage crew moves in the darkness putting together our set, I pull my wife close and tell her I will see her soon and that I love her.

The curtain falls. The crowd goes into madness and we play our opening song, the first release off the album, and damn; it feels so good to be back on this stage. We wrap the first number and I stride across the floor, catching the eyes of as many in the crowd as I can. "What's going on San Diego!!"

The stadium roars, and I can feel the vibration in my chest. It's energizing in a primal way.

"We want to play something for you that you haven't heard on *Revolutionary: Volume I*. Mainly because you'll hear it on *Volume II* this fall," the guys and I laugh as I glance in the wings at Alyssa. "So, it's going to be something special for all of you! It's called, *The Dance We Do in the Dark*."

I pump my fist in the air, counting the band down, "And it goes. Like. This..."

Rah Rah! Rah Rah! Rah Rah!

Draw-ing down I find,

My facade stripp-ing away,

Falling away Taken away

You. Bend me to your will

Your presence e-nough to

Dom-i-nate and control my mind

Sha-dows give way to light

Falling away

Taken away

Sweet in-sanity!

My supp-lication is complete

But its the dance

We do-in the dark

That brings me

To

My

Knees

You bring my world

Out of

Obscurity

But its the dance

We do- in the dark.
I lay my sword- at your feet
With ev-ery word you
Whisper I heed the comm-and
Listening now Following now
I am poss-essed by you
This de-mon heart is
Yours by right
Overtaken by the light
Listening now
Following now
Sweet in-sanity!
My supp-lication is complete
But its the dance
We do-in the dark
That brings me
To
My
Knees
You bring my world
Out of
Obscurity
But its the dance
We do- in the dark.
Over-taking my heart
This man of flame
I lay my sword at your feet
But its the dance
(The dance Rah!)
We do-in the dark
(The dark Rah!)
That brings me

To

My

Knees

You bring my world

Out of

Obscurity

But its the dance

(The dance Rah!)

We do- in the dark

(The dark Rah!)

It's the dance

(It's the dance)

We do

(We do)

In the dark

About the Author

J anuary is a longtime writer and holds a BS in Sociology with an interest in Religious Studies. She is an avid reader of fantasy and science fiction and a lover of all genres of music. January is based in the wilds of the Missouri Midwest where she loves to embroider bad words on bookmarks, have cocktails and queso with her friends, and go on long walks with her husband, Jarritt.

www.januarykelly.com
Follow on Facebook:
https://www.facebook.com/profile.php?id=100067850730415
Instagram:
https://www.instagram.com/januarykelly.author/?next=%2F

Also By

Paranormal Romantic Suspense, The Hidden Series:
The Night They Knew- a short story from The Hidden
Hidden Intent
Smoke and Shadow
Relative Deceit
Standalone:
The Last Lament of the Late Shawn Reilly
Contemporary Fiction
All These Days
Romantic Suspense
Dangerous Flame
All The Reasons I Love You
Judas, Sinful Salvation Book 1 [A collaboration with Amanda East]

JANUARY
KELLY